When Black Dogs Sing

In memory of our beautiful mother,
Patsy

For Lesley-Ann,
Thanks so much for your support!
best wishes,
Tanya x

Tanya Farrelly

When Black Dogs Sing

When Black Dogs Sing

is published in 2016 by
ARLEN HOUSE
42 Grange Abbey Road
Baldoyle
Dublin 13
Ireland
Phone/Fax: 353 86 8207617
Email: arlenhouse@gmail.com
arlenhouse.blogspot.com

Distributed internationally by
SYRACUSE UNIVERSITY PRESS
621 Skytop Road, Suite 110
Syracuse, NY 13244–5290
Phone: 315–443–5534/Fax: 315–443–5545
Email: supress@syr.edu

978–1–85132–147–6, paperback

Typesetting by Arlen House

Cover art 'Vaudeville' and 'Odalisque' by David Sweet
are reproduced courtesy of the artist
www.davidsweet.co.uk

Contents

When Black Dogs Sing

When Black Dogs Sing

Carla stands in the back yard and stares up at the sky. Occasionally, the clouds part to reveal a sliver of moon. It casts its light on the wooden fence that separates Carla's vegetable patch from the rest of the yard, but mostly the clouds cover the sky and it is impossible to see the surroundings. For Carla, this is not a problem. She knows every inch of this land, the position of every tree and where the earth is uneven. She walks it every night and doesn't need the moonlight to guide her.

As Carla stands there she smokes a cigarette. The smoke spirals upwards towards the cloudy sky. She puts out a hand and absently strokes the black dog that stands by her side, black as the night that surrounds them.

'Where is he, Bobby?' she says. 'Where's my boy?'

The dog pushes his face into her hand. She feels the dampness of his nose, his rough tongue as he slides it along her palm. She runs her hand along his back, buries her fingers in his thick fur and feels him pressing against her.

In the shed, Carla turns on the light. Sheila lifts her head off the blanket in her bed and looks at Carla with tired eyes. Six black pups nuzzle her body. Their tiny paws press into her stomach as they squirm and nibble, pawing and clawing at each other in an attempt to get their mother's milk. Every so often, she pushes them away roughly with her nose.

Carla kneels down and rubs Sheila's ears. She looks at the pups. Some of them are sleeping, the others constantly move depriving the older dog of sleep.

'Don't worry girl, I won't touch them', she says. She knows the protective instinct of this mother for her young.

Carla turns out the light, steps outside and pushes a brick against the door to keep it ajar. Slowly, she walks back towards the house, the black dog at her side, his paws softly beating a rhythm on the pathway through the grass.

A light burns in the kitchen. Carla pictures Ray inside. She hears the tap running and guesses that he's making a last pot of tea before going to bed. It's strange, him being here. His coat hanging on the end of the banister, his boots beneath the stairs where they used to be. She stops in the hall and looks at them, farmers' boots, mud caked into the soles and sides; tracks on the lino where he came in from the yard.

The kitchen is warm. He stands at the sink scalding the teapot. He turns as he hears her come in.

'Will you have a drop of tea?' he says.

'Sure why not'.

She sits at the kitchen table. The dog lies at her foot. She takes a digestive biscuit from the packet, breaks it in two and gives him half. He arrived three months ago. They had been alerted to his presence by late-night howling on the doorstep. She put up posters around the neighbourhood, but no one had claimed him and Lucas begged her to keep him. The dog developed an allegiance to Carla and had followed her ever since.

She watches as Ray takes two mugs out of the press, his back to her. He knows where everything's kept. Why wouldn't he? It was his home for almost ten years. It feels like a lifetime ago.

'Any news?' Ray asks.

He sits opposite her, pours tea into her mug and then his own. She shakes her head and looks away so that he doesn't see the fear in her eyes. She knows it has been there lately. She's seen it as she's stood in front of the mirror undressing for bed, trying to block out the voices telling her that Lucas might never come home.

Ray sighs, lifts the mug to his lips and drinks loudly. For a short time they sit in silence, each one afraid to voice their fears. When he arrived three weeks before they had sat at this table and she had told him everything she could about the last time she had seen their son. He'd made suggestions, the two of them carrying out their own investigation that always led to the same place. Nowhere.

'Have you been up at the Reynolds' place?' Ray puts his mug down and looks straight at her.

'I've been outside checking on the dogs'.

'You know you can't keep doing this, Carla'.

'I'm not doing anything', she says, but she doesn't look at him when she speaks.

'Tom Reynolds told me that you've been going up there. That he's seen you standing outside the house at night'.

She says nothing.

'He says it'll have to stop. That he doesn't know anything about Lucas'.

'He didn't just disappear, Ray'. Her voice trembles.

'You can't go accusing innocent people'.

'Why not?' she says.

He sighs, exasperated, and a small, rational part of her knows that there is some truth in what he's saying, that she has no idea what has happened to their son.

'He felt bad telling me. He said he can't imagine what we must be going through, but you can't go prying into other people's lives, Carla'.

She looks at the ground. 'You must think I'm crazy', she says.

'No'. Ray stands up and rinses his mug at the sink. He pauses as he walks past, squeezes her shoulder and she almost puts a hand up to touch his. She raises it a little and then lets it fall in her lap again.

Upstairs, Carla hears him bumping around in Lucas's room. She imagines him getting undressed, sitting on the edge of the bed, looking around at his son's things and knowing that he doesn't belong there. She pictures him spinning the globe on Lucas's desk, jabbing it with his finger and wondering where on the earth his son could be.

Carla sits there and drains the last of her tea. She glances in the bottom of the cup where the tea-leaves are scattered in an uneven pattern. Her grandmother used to read these. She remembers women coming to the house in the hope of uncovering their fortunes. She'd never believed in such things. Still doesn't. She doesn't believe that some gypsy woman can reveal the whereabouts of her son, but she is almost desperate enough to try.

Overhead, the bumping gives way to silence. Ray has gone to bed. She stands up, slowly, rinses the mug and hangs it on the wooden stand. She takes the black dog's lead from a drawer and he rises knowing that it's time.

The torch bobs as she walks, its milky beam illuminating the hedges at the sides of the narrow road. The dog pulls ahead, his breathing fast and rasping in the night air. She walks quickly, her footsteps making no sound in her canvas shoes. She keeps to the middle of the country road.

She has no fear of traffic. Few cars pass this way and she will see their lights as soon as they turn the bend at the top of the hill. The night is thick around them. They push on, the dog leading the woman through the night.

Eventually, he slows down. He stops every now and then to smell at the edge of the ditch, pricks up his ears when he hears a rustling in the hedges. Carla listens too. She knows that it's a creature, maybe a rat scurrying through the muddy waters, but every time the dog stops to sniff the air her heart quickens and she tries not to picture her son's body, cold and muddied, lying at the bottom of the ditch covered by brambles.

Every night, the woman and the dog trace the boy's footsteps. She knows that whatever happened, happened along this stretch of road, the half-mile between their house and the Reynolds'. They have combed the area, search teams with sniffer-dogs, they've spoken to all the residents in a ten-mile radius and they have uncovered nothing. Not one person saw Lucas walking to the Reynolds' house that evening.

Carla and the dog stop at the end of the laneway that leads onto Tom Reynolds' land. His red jeep is parked outside the garage. She stands there and watches the house in silence, the dog motionless by her side. The curtains are open and she can see into the living room. Reynolds' wife is there sitting in front of the television. She is alone. There is no sign of Reynolds himself or of the boy. Every time she sees him, she feels a tightness in her throat that makes it difficult to breathe. If it weren't for the boy, she thinks, Lucas wouldn't have taken that road.

Carla hears a noise. She stands back, crouches down low, her hand steady on the dog's lead. She presses his back gently and he lies down beside her. Tom Reynolds appears from around the side of the house. His son walks behind him. He opens the back door of the jeep and the boy stands there quietly. Carla strains to see what they're doing. She hears her pulse hammering in her ears. He takes something from the back of the jeep, but she is too far away to see what it is. He slams the door shut and leads his son to the garage. He shifts the door and gestures for him to enter. The boy walks inside, his head down. She hears voices. They have vanished from view now. She thinks she hears a boy whimpering and she moves forward instinctively, every nerve-end taut.

She keeps to the shadows of the trees, grips the dog's lead tightly. She is afraid of what she might see inside, but she is determined to find out what has happened to her son. It is dark in the garage. Reynolds has left the light off. She creeps nearer. She is within feet of the door now. The whimpering continues, but it is not the voice of her son. In a corner at the back of the garage, she sees Reynolds. He is crouching over something. Someone.

'No, Dad, please!'

Reynolds' son's voice is a whisper.

'I won't say anything, I promise, Dad. Please don't'.

He is crying now. Reynolds doesn't say anything. She hears the clink of his belt buckle as he removes it from his trousers and she stands there unable to move. As the leather cracks on the boy's back, he yells out in pain. The black dog shifts at her side and a low growl escapes his lips. Carla hushes him, her mouth close to his ear.

She stands up, her legs shaking. She considers rushing into the garage to stop this hideous beating, but who knows what Reynolds might do. The only way she can save the boy is to get away from this place, to tell someone what she has seen. They will have to believe her now. They will have to help her to find Lucas.

As they walk up the lane approaching her house, Carla sees a figure at the gate. Her heart quickens. For a moment she wonders if Reynolds saw her after all, if he decided to follow her here, took a shortcut through the fields to reach the house before she arrived. She takes the black dog off the lead, expecting him to rush forward. Instead he continues to walk at the same pace.

'Where've you been, Carla?'

Ray's voice rings out clear in the night. He stands at the gate looking out across the land and she almost runs to reach him. She tries to speak, to tell him about Reynolds, but instead the tears come, hot and fast, and she knows, as sure as the black dog will continue to walk by her side, that Lucas will never come home.

Exposed

'Rita-Lynn. What kind of a name's that?' Darragh asked. 'Sounds like a country singer'.

We were hauling boxes from the back of my old Micra, books spilling from crates that I'd borrowed from the local supermarket and loading them up in Rita-Lynn's hall. In the past week, I'd been to see half a dozen places – some of them cramped or damp or obscenely overpriced, so when I met Rita-Lynn and she showed me the spacious room in her two-bed duplex, I figured my problems had ended.

We half-placed, half-dropped another crate beneath the stairs.

'Just those two cases and I think we're done. Give us the keys and I'll lock her up'.

I tossed Darragh the keys, a half-smile on my lips.

'What's up with you?' he said.

I shook my head, grinning. 'Nothing, just happy'. I blew him a kiss, and he winked and disappeared to get the last of my things.

Sidestepping the crates piled round my feet, I pushed open the door to the living room. 'Jesus, I'm sorry. I ... I didn't think you were here'.

Clutching the door handle, I stood transfixed at the scene before me. Rita-Lynn, wearing a garish orange dress, was crouched before a longhaired man who was entirely naked. She didn't turn at the interruption, but moved round her subject, camera pointed, eye to the lens, shutter clicking. The man gazed at the far wall and showed no sign that he was even aware of the interruption.

I turned when I felt Darragh come up behind me. He raised an eyebrow and laughter stirred deep in my belly at the look on his face. I half-shoved him out of the room, uttering a further apology before closing the door behind us. We hadn't reached my room before we both erupted in hilarity. I shushed Darragh, opened the door and fell on the bed in hysterics.

'What the hell was that?' he said.

I held my stomach, laughter bubbling inside me. 'Rita, she's a ...' I couldn't finish and it was another few minutes before I managed to splutter the word 'photographer'.

'So this is what it's going to like around here, is it? Naked guys in the living room ... hmm, I think I ought to take you to Cork with me after all'. Darragh smiled and started to tickle me. I attempted to fend him off.

'I told you she was a bit of an eccentric, but I like her. She's ...'

'Another arty layabout, right up your street'. He pinned me to the bed by the wrists and tickled me till I screamed for mercy.

Darragh liked to tease me about my friends – often referring to them as the psychedelic bunch, though none of them used drugs. I sometimes wondered if I wasn't too alternative for him. My passion lay in the arts. At university I'd studied drama and contemporary dance.

And I'd just started a night course in reiki healing. Darragh was fanatical about running and the GAA. He talked politics and economics and all the things I'd found dull before I met him. For his sake I tried to brush up on my obsolete knowledge of hurling and football and he agreed to be dragged along to the theatre once a month, as well as hanging out with my bohemian friends. Whatever our differences we were crazy about each other.

Darragh had been offered a position lecturing in criminal justice in UCC a few months previous. He hadn't been happy in the law firm he'd been working for in Dublin and decided that this was a position he couldn't turn down. I was upset at first; I knew it wouldn't take much to lure him back to his native Cork. But he promised to return to Dublin at weekends and so far he'd kept his word.

That evening after we'd hauled all my stuff up to my room, I dropped Darragh to the train station. 'Stay away from those naked photo shoots', he told me, grinning – and we kissed goodbye as the train pulled in.

By the time I arrived back it had got dark. The light was on in the hall and music was playing in the living room. Rita-Lynn stuck her head out the door as I was taking off my coat. 'How do you fancy a Chinese this evening to celebrate your moving in?' she asked.

'Yeah, that'd be great'. I followed her into the living room where tea light candles were scattered round the room bathing it in a soft light. She was barefoot, still wearing the orange dress. Her naked guest had departed.

'Sorry about earlier, I didn't mean to barge in ...'

Rita-Lynn snorted. 'Don't worry, Tony didn't mind. Probably enjoyed it, truth be told'.

She threw a couple of cushions on the floor, went out of the room and returned with two sets of chopsticks and a menu for the local Chinese takeaway.

'Is he your boyfriend?' I asked.

'Tony? Jesus, no! I met him at a tango class a few months back. What would you like?'

She handed me the menu, and we decided on a set meal for two.

Half an hour later, sitting cross-legged on the floor with trays of food spread on the table between us, Rita-Lynn told me about the men in her life – and about the recent break-up with her fiancé that had led to her advertising the room.

'I finished it two weeks before the wedding', she said. 'The closer it got, the more I knew I couldn't go through with it. I'd started having anxiety attacks – waking in the night unable to breathe. I've always suffered from them, but this was bad. Although maybe it wasn't all that bad. If it weren't for the anxiety I might have gone through with it. It's like a trigger, lets me know when something's not right. More wine?'

Rita-Lynn held the bottle over my glass and I nodded.

'How did you tell him?'

'I just said it straight out. Eamon – that's his name – he was in the bedroom – reading. I just went in and told him I couldn't do it'.

'What did he say?'

'He looked up from his book and asked me if I was sure. I told him I was. The next day when I came home from work, he'd gone'.

'Have you ever regretted it?'

She shook her head. 'For months before it ended, I'd had to force myself to have sex with him. When I told him about it, you know what he said? That he'd felt the same. It was dead for him too'. She took a long sip of her wine – then looked directly at me. 'How many men have you slept with?' she asked.

I laughed, embarrassed. 'Darragh's the third'.

Rita-Lynn looked at me, an anticipatory smile on her lips. 'I've slept with twenty-six', she said.

'Seriously?'

'I need sex. It's ... a form of therapy. It keeps me sane'.

I felt part-horrified, part-intrigued by my flatmate's disclosure.

'I can't sleep with someone I'm not in love with', I told her. 'It has to really mean something for me'.

Rita-Lynn pushed her plate away, sat back and looked at me.

'Come on, Lisa. Haven't you ever wanted to do something for pleasure? For curiosity's sake? I slept with a woman once. I went to a gay bar and this woman came up to me. She wasn't beautiful – but I went home with her, just to know what it was like'.

If she'd wanted to shock me, she had. The food I'd eaten lay heavy in my stomach.

'It was good', she continued. 'Lasted a few weeks. She was the one who finished it. Dropped me for an ex, some dykey type'.

'So, you're ... bisexual?'

She shook her head and smiled. 'No, like I said, just curious'.

Rita-Lynn went out that night. When she was gone I went up to my room and lay on the bed to read. I thought about what she'd told me – it had taken some courage to call off the wedding. Eamon, the fiancé, must have been devastated, but better she'd done it before rather than after the event. I fell asleep on top of the duvet not having read a word and woke later that night to the sound of voices in the hallway. There was a bump, followed by Rita's stifled laughter, then a man's voice, low and reassuring. I wondered if it were Tony, the tango dancer. I undressed, climbed into bed and lay sleepless, trying not to listen to the sounds from the next room.

Darragh didn't take to Rita. He thought she was coarse and said it wouldn't be any harm if she ran a brush through her hair once in a while. There was something else too, he said, something not right about her – in the head.

'Since when are you are the psychologist?' I asked him.

'It wouldn't take a psychologist to know there's something off about your flatmate', he said.

It was true that Rita-Lynn was obscene. Her stories were designed to shock and she had a voracious need for attention. She liked nothing better than to provoke her audience, something that embarrassed me in Darragh's presence, but on the nights he was away, Rita-Lynn often regaled me with her squalid tales.

I'd been living with Rita-Lynn two months when I experienced her anxiety first-hand. I came home one evening to find her white-faced and trembling because she couldn't get the TV to switch on.

'Rita, what's wrong? Are you ok?' I put my hand on her shoulder.

She was breathing hard, one hand clutching at her throat. She pushed her unruly hair back from her face. 'I … I can't get it to work. It just won't come on. I've tried everything'.

'Here give it to me'. I took the remote control from her and pressed the buttons. Nothing happened. I crossed the room to the TV and pressed the button. The green light came on and the television fizzed to life. 'The batteries are gone in the remote'.

Rita-Lynn sat down, head in her hands. 'My heart's thumping', she said. I sat next to her and stroked her hair. She lifted her head, eyes closed. 'That's so calming. Don't stop. You're giving me ASMR'.

'ASM …?'

'Autonomous Sensory Meridian Response. You can get it from different things. Sometimes when I hear you talking, I get it. It's just this calm, tingling sensation … there are videos about it on Youtube'.

Rita's breathing slowed as I stroked her hair. After a few minutes she turned to me and smiled. 'Thanks', she said. 'Technology always does that to me. I can't stand it'.

'Have you ever tried reiki?' I asked.

Rita-Lynn shook her head. 'Is it a course for technophobes?'

I laughed. 'No, it's a type of holistic healing. I'm doing a night course in it at the moment. It's really good for stress. If you were willing, you could be my guinea pig?'

Rita-Lynn smiled. 'Ok. But in turn you have to let me take your photo'.

She stuck out her hand and, after a moment's hesitation, I shook on it.

Darragh didn't come home that weekend. There was a match on, so he was staying with his brother. 'Do you mind, baby?' he said. I said I didn't, but it was Thursday evening and I'd been looking forward to seeing him the next day. 'We'll do something special to make up for it, I promise', he told me. I hung up, slightly annoyed that he'd left it till the last minute to tell me his plans. He must have known for at least a week.

'No Darragh tonight?' Rita-Lynn said.

It was Saturday evening. I was sitting watching a DVD in the living room. 'No, he stayed down to go to a match with his brother'.

She sat down next to me on the couch. 'What are you watching?'

'*Midnight in Paris*'.

She nodded. 'I was supposed to go to a French film at the IFI, but my friend cancelled. Is this on long?'

'Yeah, it's nearly over. If you wanted we could watch something else. I've seen it before anyway'.

Rita-Lynn picked up the remote control and turned off the television. 'I have a better idea. How about you do some of that reiki stuff on me? I could do with something to help me de-stress'.

A few minutes later Rita-Lynn was lying face down on the couch. 'How long have you been with Darragh?' Her voice was muffled against the seat.

'Seven, nearly eight months'. I laid my hands on her shoulders.

'And do you trust him?'

'Of course, why do you ask?'

'I don't trust any man', she said. 'Not since what happened with Eamon'.

'Eamon, your ex? But didn't you leave him?'

'Yeah, but only after I'd found out he'd been with someone else'.

'I thought you said it had worn off, that you just didn't feel the same about him'.

'Well, I didn't. I mean would you, if you'd found out something like that? Don't tell me you believe there's any man would refuse it if a half-decent girl were to offer it to them, no strings attached?' She squirmed and twisted to look at me.

'Turn around, I'm not done yet', I said. I rested my hands on the small of her back.

'There are plenty of guys like that but I also know a lot of guys who wouldn't sleep with just anyone, that aren't just interested in sex'.

Rita-Lynn harrumphed. She was in a strange mood that evening and it was beginning to irritate me.

'Well, I admire your faith in mankind', she said. 'Can't say I share it. If you ask me they'd all succumb if you put them to the test. The thing is most people don't because they don't want to know the truth'.

Reiki didn't seem to have much of an effect on Rita-Lynn – probably because she talked through most sessions when she should've been lying quietly. By then I'd discovered that the simplest things triggered her angst. It was Darragh who rescued her from her next full-blown attack. Though this one, it seemed, was warranted.

Darragh had come up every weekend since the hurling match. His team had, to my secret joy, been knocked out. That Friday he didn't have any classes so he'd got the early train to Dublin, arriving a good hour before I got in from work. He hadn't expected to walk into the living room to find Rita-Lynn crying in what he described as near hysterics. By the time I arrived the episode had passed, but the evidence remained. Rita-Lynn was sitting on the couch, black mascara rubbed down her face. Since when had she worn mascara? Now that I noticed, she'd also had her hair dyed and cut. The boisterous black curls had been straightened and hung sleek round her face.

'Hey, what's going on?'

Darragh gave me a look, but waited for Rita-Lynn to answer.

She rubbed her eyes again, extending the damage. 'I was in town. I went in to meet some people for a photography shoot and I saw Eamon. He was with some girl, his arm around her shoulder walking through Temple Bar'.

I sat on the arm of Darragh's chair. 'I'm sorry'.

Rita-Lynn sniffed and rubbed her nose with the back of her hand. 'I suppose I shouldn't be that surprised, it was bound to happen. It was a shock seeing him with someone else, you know?' She turned to Darragh. 'Sorry Darragh, I didn't mean for you to walk in on me like that. You must think I'm nuts'.

'No. You … you got a shock. It's understandable'.

Darragh looked at me, and turned back to Rita-Lynn.

'Look, we were planning on ordering a take-away and watching a movie. Do you want to join us?'

Rita-Lynn looked at me.

'Do you mind? I wouldn't be in the way or anything? I don't want to go spoiling your plans'.

'No. It would be fun. Let's do that'. I smiled at Darragh, knowing that it wasn't the evening he'd planned. He was more tolerant of Rita-Lynn after that. I guess every man softens to a woman in distress.

'Just a minute, I want to get the lighting right'. Rita-Lynn adjusted the lights as I sat on a high stool before the white blind and waited to have my photo taken. Unlike Tony, the tango dancer, I was fully clothed. Rita-Lynn had called me out on our deal.

'You have such good features', she said. Before the shoot she'd insisted on doing my make-up. My lids were smudged black, kohl outlining the contours of my eyes so that they glittered cobalt blue. She'd run a brush along my jaw heightening my cheekbones. My lips were coated nude.

Rita-Lynn observed me, satisfied that the lights were right. Then, eye to the lens, she captured my image. I had the sudden giddy thought that she was stealing my soul. She had me turn my head at different angles – shutter snapping. 'Beautiful', she said.

'How many pictures do you plan on taking?'

She'd stopped to study the shots that she'd done. 'Just a few more, maybe something a bit … sexier'.

I laughed nervously. 'What exactly do you have in mind?'

'What about topless, but from the back? It won't show anything. The back is one of the most beautiful parts of the body'.

'No way', I said. 'What if you showed them to someone?'

'I won't. I swear. If you like them, you can keep them. And if you don't, I'll delete them. Might be a nice present for Darragh'.

I looked at her, doubtful, but the idea had already begun to appeal to me. What would I look like through Rita-Lynn's eyes?

The shots were tasteful. Me with my back to the camera, looking over my shoulder, hair swept back from my face. As the shutter clicked, I became more daring, turning slightly to the side, I allowed her to capture me, the contour of my breast semi-revealed. She had me sit astride the stool; a floppy hat perched atop my head – a white blouse, unbuttoned. I'd never done anything so daring. I imagined Darragh scandalised by such abandon and vowed not to show him the shots. I would keep them some place he wouldn't find them.

Rita-Lynn printed the pictures that evening. She came to my room, envelope in her hand and a big grin on her face. By that time the giddiness that'd seized me during the shoot had dissipated and I was beginning to think that it hadn't been my greatest idea. But the shots *were* good. Rita-Lynn sat on the edge of the bed and went through them. The girl in the photographs looked, in turn, bold, playful and confident. She knew that I was neurotic about it so when we'd finished we went to her room and she deleted the file from her computer whilst I watched, leaving me with the hardcopies.

'Now, you won't have to worry about any accidental uploading on Facebook', she said.

I punched her arm. 'Don't even joke about it'.

Back in my room I put the envelope in a shoebox on top of the wardrobe where I kept old pictures and letters. That afternoon's activity was to be my and Rita-Lynn's secret.

I completed the reiki course and the reiki master put me in touch with a friend of his who ran a holistic healing centre. The woman offered me a few hours a couple of evenings each week, unpaid, on a trial basis. It was on the other side of the city but I was happy to get the experience. With Rita-Lynn's permission, I'd given Darragh a key to the apartment as it was often ten o'clock by the time I got home on a Friday. Darragh didn't mind. He entertained himself watching television until I arrived. He'd been getting on well with Rita-Lynn since the anxiety incident and, though he still maintained there was something off about her, he'd become more tolerant of her outrageous behaviour.

I arrived one Friday night, tired and soaked from the walk from the bus, to find Rita-Lynn sitting alone in the living room.

'Darragh upstairs?' I asked.

She shook her head.

I looked at my watch. 'That's odd. His train must've been delayed'.

She looked at me. 'He left'.

'Left? Why?' I looked at my phone as I asked and discovered I'd forgotten to take it off silent when I'd left the centre. There were two missed calls – both Darragh, less than ten minutes before.

'I don't know how to tell you this. Look …' Rita-Lynn began.

'Go on'.

'Darragh tried to kiss me'.

I was halfway out of my wet coat. I stared at Rita-Lynn who was sitting hands between her knees looking straight at me. 'What are you talking about? Darragh wouldn't ... there's obviously been some misunderstanding'.

She took a deep breath. 'Maybe I shouldn't have told you, but you're my friend. I'd never forgive myself ... I mean if it were me, I'd ...'

'I think you'd better explain what you think happened here'.

'He arrived earlier than usual. I was in the kitchen tidying up and we got talking. He asked me if I was ok now after the Eamon situation – and ... well, we were talking and then he leaned in and kissed me'.

'He kissed you?'

'I pulled away, of course, asked him what he thought he was doing. He got embarrassed then, asked me not to tell you. I got a bit, well, hysterical, shouted at him to leave. And he did. I'm so sorry, Lisa'.

I had my phone to my ear dialling into my voicemail before she'd even finished. I had two new messages. The first was blank. The second, Darragh, telling me in the brusquest of tones to call him – that he needed to talk to me about 'that bitch Rita-Lynn'.

I stood there staring at Rita-Lynn. She was looking at me pityingly. 'I need to talk to Darragh', I said.

She clutched at my arm, eyes widening in panic. 'Don't believe anything he says, he'll try to wheedle his way out of it', she told me. 'At least you know now what he's like'.

I shook Rita-Lynn off my arm and marched up to my room. Darragh answered on the second ring. 'Has that bitch been telling her lies?' he said. 'Don't believe anything she says. I told you there's something wrong with her, Lee. Well, now she's gone and proved it'.

'Where are you?'

'I called over to Mike's. I'll come and meet you, but not there. Not with her'.

'Right, look we'll meet in Thomas Read's. I can be there in half an hour'.

It was quiet for a Friday. I took a seat at the window at the back of the bar and waited for Darragh to arrive. Rita-Lynn had phoned me after I'd left the house, but I hadn't answered. I needed to hear what Darragh had to say. At that moment I didn't know what to think. Would she have made it up? Was she capable of it? I couldn't see what she'd hope to achieve. No, I refused to believe it. Believing it meant an end to everything.

Darragh arrived, soaked-through by the rain. He took off his coat and hung it on the back of the chair. For a moment he said nothing, trying to gauge my reaction.

'She's a lying fucking bitch', he said.

'What happened?'

'Not what she said, that's for sure'.

'Tell me, Darragh'.

'She started her usual, turned the tears on. I was stupid enough to be taken in by it, next thing she's all over me. I pushed her off, a bit rough maybe. And she started screaming at me. The way she was going on you'd think I'd tried to assault, not reject her. She's nuts, Lee. I told you that'.

I said nothing, trying to take it in. Had Rita-Lynn looked like she'd been crying? I didn't recall her eyes looking red.

Darragh's eyes narrowed. 'You do believe me?' he said.

'I want to'.

'You want to? You mean you'd even think of taking her word over mine?' He turned his anger on me. 'Are you for real, Lee? I thought we had something serious here, but maybe I was wrong. If you could doubt my word and believe that ... that ...' He trailed off, his eyes full of disgust. He went to pick up his coat.

I put my hand on his arm. 'No, Darragh. I do. I do believe you ... just think for a minute what this is like for me. I mean, why would she say that? We're friends'.

Darragh shrugged. This time he did put on his coat. 'Some friend. Maybe she has a thing for you and wants to split us up. I don't know'.

I coloured at his words. I hadn't told Darragh about Rita's bi admission. I didn't know why, but at the time I didn't want to give him ammunition against her. Besides, it wasn't quite the admission; she'd said it had been a curiosity, nothing more.

I thought of the photo shoot and wondered if there was any truth in Darragh's suggestion. Glad that I'd never been tempted to show him the shots, I vowed to get rid of them as soon as I got home.

'Look, this is the last thing I want to do', he said, 'but if you want we can go there now and I'll tell you in front of her that this is a pack of lies'.

'No. There's no need for that. I know you're not lying. I just can't understand why she'd do this. Is there any way she could have misunderstood?'

Darragh shook his head. 'There was nothing I said that could have encouraged her'.

'Well, there's nothing for it. I'll have to move out. I can't stay living there now, after this'.

Darragh nodded. 'I won't be setting foot there again, you can be sure of that'.

I moved out of Rita-Lynn's apartment the following weekend. We'd been avoiding each other and when we did happen to enter the same room, the atmosphere was taut. Darragh took a couple of days off so that he could help me with the crates when Rita-Lynn was at work. He said he never wanted to have to see her again. I hadn't found an apartment yet, but my sister had offered to put me up until I did.

That Sunday afternoon, I tapped on the living room door to return the key to Rita-Lynn. She turned off the television and stood up when I entered. She took the keys that I held out to her.

'I wish this'd never happened', she said. I nodded. A part of me wished that she'd apologise and things could return to how they'd been before. 'What I told you was true, Lisa'. She held my stare – I noticed she'd reverted to not wearing make-up. There were circles under her eyes.

'Goodbye, Rita', I said.

For the first few weeks, I worried about whether Rita-Lynn had saved copies of those pictures she'd taken. She'd tagged me in a photo on Facebook and when I saw the notification my heart almost failed. I opened it to find that it was a quote about friendship – the background was a black-and-white shot of two girls embracing. I ignored it. Some things cannot be undone.

I rented an apartment on the northside, close to where the reiki clinic was located. My new flatmate, a girl called Eileen, was a doctor and was rarely home. Darragh was glad that I'd found someone 'without issues' to live with. He'd never forgive Rita-Lynn.

Darragh continued to come up to Dublin at weekends. And then he didn't. I'd been living in the new apartment about six weeks when he called to say that he was staying down for a football match. The All-Ireland had started and I'd braced myself for his absence. The following Wednesday evening, he sent a text: 'Table booked. Seeya at 7pm. XXX'. I stared at the screen. What was he talking about? We hadn't made plans. I felt, suddenly, ill. I considered calling him, but what would I say? I didn't reply to the text and when we spoke, he didn't mention it.

I sat outside the station waiting to pick him up. When I saw him come out, his sports bag slung over his shoulder, I almost faltered. He opened the door. 'Hey beautiful'. I stared at him trying to spot anything different. He noticed and asked what was wrong.

'Have a nice dinner on Wednesday night?' I asked.

He hesitated – then started to look annoyed. 'What are you talking about, Lisa?' His accent had got stronger. It always did when he was annoyed.

'Why didn't you just tell me, Darragh, instead of being such a coward?'

He faked an amazed look. 'What exactly is it that I'm supposed to have done here?' he asked.

I was trembling. 'You sent me the text'.

'What text?'

'About booking a restaurant'.

He shook his head. 'That was for Paul. We had dinner before the match'.

I nodded. 'Usually put kisses on Paul's texts, do you?'

'Alright, Lisa. It was a friend, ok. I was meeting a friend. I knew I couldn't tell you. You've always been irrational about these things'.

I leaned across him and opened the door. 'Irrational?' I snorted. 'I should have listened to Rita-Lynn when it came to you'. I took his bag and flung it out the door. 'You can go to hell, Darragh'.

'No, you can, Lisa. You can'.

His face was red with fury. He got out and slammed the door.

I watched as he strode back to the station in the rain. He didn't turn his head as he disappeared through the double doors. For a few minutes I sat watching the rain trickle down the windscreen, then I picked up the phone and rang Rita-Lynn.

THE PRODIGAL

My brother has come home after an absence of seven years. His tall, thin frame hovers in the doorway, an unlit cigarette dangling between his tobacco-stained fingers as his eyes flick about the room and focus on nothing in particular. I can't help but wonder if he's noticed the absence of ceremony that accompanies his return. There are no colourful balloons strung from the balustrade, no welcome-home banner brushes the top of Christian's head as he enters our living room. Instead his return is met with anxious glances and too-bright smiles. My voice is an octave too loud and betrays that this is not the kind of reunion that I desire.

Christian's been clutching that cigarette since he got into the car. Reason tells me that he's dying to light it, but that he's too polite or preoccupied to ask. As he enters the room I find myself babbling about the new decking that we got earlier in the summer. I swing open the back door, forgetting about Jess, our five-month-old collie, who flies at the newcomer before he's even got through the door. Christian puts the cigarette in his mouth and stoops to fondle the dog's ears, relieved perhaps by the first genuine greeting he's received all day. And I remember that my brother has always loved dogs and that each dog we've ever had has sworn its allegiance to him. I look at Jess now feeling slightly betrayed and question her judgement of character.

'I don't suppose you've a light?' The cigarette jigs up and down as Christian speaks.

'Matter of fact I do', I say. 'Barry's a chain-smoker'.

I return to the kitchen and stand on the first rung of a stool to retrieve a lighter from the top shelf of the cupboard where we keep it out of Emily's reach. I've learned over the years what not to leave around a small child. When I get down from the stool I linger in the kitchen and watch as my brother picks up a stone and, with a deft movement of the wrist, sends it hurtling down the garden. Jess barks and bounds after it, skidding to a halt by the gazebo. She looks back and pants happily at her new friend, her mouth open in what looks like a wide grin.

I toss Christian the lighter and tell him that I'll show him his room when he's ready. I stand behind my brother for a few minutes, but he doesn't say anything and I go back inside to start the evening meal, leaving him leaning over the decking puffing on his cigarette with the dog prostrate at his feet.

The light has faded by the time Christian comes in. I'm at the sink peeling and chopping vegetables and I don't hear him come up behind me. When I turn and see him standing close by I give a start and then laugh to try to conceal my all-too-real anxiety.

'I didn't hear you come in', I say.

Christian ignores my uneasiness and asks if he can help with something.

I wipe my hands on the tea towel, smile broadly and tell him that everything's under control.

He stands close to me and I get the faint smell of perspiration rising from beneath his thin cotton shirt.

'Come on, I'll show you where you're sleeping'. I give him a wide berth as I pass and he follows me like the collie to the bottom of the stairs.

In Emily's room, I reach for the light. Christian looks around, I see him take in the dolls' house, the army of stuffed toys, button eyes glowing in the harsh electric light, and Emily's Hanna Montana posters pinned to the wall. He puts his bag at the end of the bed and runs a hand over the soft pink quilt.

'I hope you don't mind sleeping in Emily's room', I say. 'We'd nowhere else to put you'.

Christian shakes his head. 'And what about Emily?' he asks.

'She'll sleep in with us. God knows, she does it most nights anyway'.

I tell him about my daughter's fear of the dark and he says that she must take after her mother, reminding me that I was always afraid of the monsters that lurked beneath the bed. He pats the quilt, sits unmoving and waits for me to leave. I tell him that I'll leave him to settle in, but in the doorway I pause and turn.

'Christian, I *am* sorry about Helen', I say.

He nods and his eyes look glassy.

Christian is still upstairs when Barry and Emily come home. I hear the front door opening and the sound of Emily's black patent shoes running on the wooden floor. Too late, I discover that Emily has gone straight upstairs to her room where the guest is. I call after her, but she doesn't hear or chooses to ignore me. She knows that her Uncle Christian has come to stay.

Barry kisses me in the hallway. 'How's it going?' he says and brushes the hair away from my face.

I shrug. 'Ok, I guess. The dog likes him'.

We listen for sounds from upstairs. I hear Emily squeal with laughter and I exchange a look with Barry before hurrying up the stairs. The scene when I push open Emily's bedroom door catapults me back to the past and leaves me reeling.

Emily has been introducing Christian to her family of bears and Christian, crouched on the floor, is putting on a show. He puts on a deep bear voice and Emily squeals with delight and claps her hands. He looks up and smiles when he sees me and I try to smile back, but I feel as though my face has been botoxed into position and what's supposed to be a smile passes off as a grimace as I recall the nights that Christian put on these shows for me, my beloved big brother.

Briskly, I shove off the memory.

'Emily, don't be bothering your Uncle Christian', I say, as I put my hands on my child's shoulders and swing her into a standing position.

'She's no bother', Christian says, easily. 'We were just getting to know each other a little bit, weren't we?'

I don't know if I've imagined it or if his eyes hold some kind of challenge.

Emily is playing on the living room floor. She's scattered her new set of crayons all around her and is busy transforming a ballerina elephant into a shocking shade of pink in the latest bumper colouring book that Barry bought her. She is careful to keep the colour inside the lines.

'I just don't know if this was such a good idea', I say. My voice is low. I'm aware of Christian in the room overhead and of Emily sitting nearby. I walk round the table, laying cutlery in each place and putting napkins in the glasses. Then I take the napkins out again and flatten them. This is not a celebration.

'Come on. He's just lost his wife, Jen. He needs support ... family ... I couldn't imagine losing you like that'.

'Yes, but ... it's been a long time. We didn't exactly part on the best of terms, you know?'

'Well, no, I don't really. You never said much about him. I just assumed you weren't close ... or maybe that you resented his going away a little'.

I look at Barry who is so unshakable and I wonder what he would do if I were to tell him the truth.

'His going away ... no, it wasn't that ... it's true, Helen and I never really got along, but it was nothing to do with the move ... it wasn't that. It's more complicated. It's Christian himself. He's not, he's not who people think he is. He's ...'

Christian clears his throat as he enters the room and I look up, already feeling the surge of blood to my face. I don't know how much he's heard.

'Mmm. Something smells good', he says. If he's heard anything, he doesn't show it.

At dinner, Christian sits opposite me, Barry on my right, and Emily to my left. Barry makes conversation, asks Christian if he likes football and if he's been following the league this year. Christian answers Barry's questions enthusiastically, cutting his steak into minute pieces, just as he did when we were children. As I watch him I wonder what his life has been like for the past seven years. I wonder with the distractions of his new life if he managed to forget the old one. If he managed to forget about me?

Suddenly, he looks up as though he's read my thoughts and his eyes, gold like an animal's, hold mine until I am forced to look away. Christian's eyes have a way of transfixing his prey.

'Uncle Christian, why do you have that name? Are you holy?'

Christian laughs as Emily swings her legs, fork gripped in her right hand and waits for an answer.

'Well, that's a question you'd have had to ask your granny', he says. 'But I don't think it was anything to do with religion, I guess she just liked the name. What do you think, Jen, am I a holy Joe?'

I colour for the second time and this time I force a smile. 'I wouldn't accuse you of that', I say.

'Meaning there are things you'd accuse me of?'

He is teasing me, but I look at him to see what kind of weight his words hold. I've always had a habit of analysing comments and coming up with explanations that occurred to no one but me.

'Uncle Christian, why did you go away?' Emily asks.

Christian's face darkens, he sits back, stretches his long legs under the table. His foot brushes mine and I withdraw as though I've been struck with a burning coal.

'I met a girl. We got married and went to Australia'.

'Where is she now?' Emily asks.

Christian's gold eyes cloud over and I jump to his rescue as I used to do when we were kids.

'That's enough now, Emily. Let Christian eat his dinner', I say.

My brother shoots me a grateful look and Barry, ever my saviour, changes the subject.

Just sitting at the same table as my brother has made swallowing a challenge. I take a gulp of water to dislodge the food that seems to have stuck halfway down my oesophagus. Christian may have lost weight in recent years, but it has only served to make him leaner, his jaw more angular, his eyes more striking. I look at my plate and try to pretend that he isn't sitting opposite me, but my brother's presence is not something that I can ignore.

After dinner, Christian offers to help me with the washing-up. We stand side by side at the sink, me with my Marigolds on, Christian with a tea towel in his hand meticulously drying each plate. The silence is palpable and I try to think of something to say, but everything that comes to mind sounds inane. I am relieved when Christian, who has saved some of his dissected steak, sets off in search of the dog. I turn the outside light on, partly so that he can see and partly so that I can see him. I stand inside the window and watch as Jess jumps and gambles round my brother's feet and he crouches down, playacting and lets her knock him to the ground.

In the next room, Barry plays with Emily. He is crawling on all fours with our child around his neck and she is laughing. And I realise as I listen to the sound of their laughter that I can never tell them about Christian and me and the things that we have done.

THE SILENCE OF SPACE

Donal Mac. I didn't recognise him at first. He stepped from a shadowy nook outside the casino in the laneway that led to Bray Dart station, hand outstretched and in his unmistakable timbre asked me to 'spare some change'. I shook my head, an embarrassed apology and moved swiftly past, not because I didn't want to give, but because all I had in my bag worth anything was my Leap card. And besides, the sudden appearance of the man had unnerved me.

Donal McMahon. It was the voice that did it. Careering towards the station, I didn't take – no, didn't have – the time to stop, seconds as I was from missing the train. I didn't see him properly, black-clothed against the equally dark wall. Had he a beard? He might have had. Dark hair short, or wearing a beanie maybe? That signature black beanie. A mural behind him advertising Time Out Amusements. But all of these things, these details, had escaped me in the seconds it had taken for my sleep-filled brain to register, to absorb. But the voice – that voice had registered alright. Donie Mac – at liberty, what – two years it must be, before his time. But what the hell was he doing begging outside a casino in Bray? Surely, they wouldn't have just let him out to go nowhere. There must be rules, provisions made? And Bray, why Bray? Could he have known, somehow, that he would find me here?

I settled into my seat, took off my woolly hat. Heat blew from under the seat scorching the backs of my legs as the train rattled out of the station. Had he recognised me? Donie. The name sounded strange, even in my mind. How would it sound if I said it out loud – letters forming between teeth and tongue as I hadn't allowed myself to do for a decade. DO-NIE. Would I choke on the second syllable as I had the afternoon they'd taken him away? And his brother, Remy, being led away by some woman – a neighbour or an aunt. Led to what? To safety, they said. Remy, the youngest. An awful thing for a child to witness, they'd said.

Donal McMahon appeared in my class in fifth year. I tried to remember if he'd been a student there before, if he'd simply merged from transition year which I'd skipped because my mother felt it was a waste of time, a doss year supposed to teach us skills. But, no, Donie had come from someplace else. A place he told me about later.

We didn't become friends right away. Nor did he choose me. Fate simply sat us next to each other – the only seat in the class free in a corner where Donal did his best to go unnoticed. But that wasn't exactly easy being Donal. I don't just mean how he looked. Apart from his height he probably wouldn't have stood out from the crowd. Six feet two inches, he was the subject of the usual adolescent jokes that tall boys suffer. 'Hey, Maccers, how are the clouds up there?' He ignored the grigging. Sometimes I wondered if he even heard it.

He didn't talk much, not even when we became close – as close as anyone could to Donal. He had other ways of expressing himself. The most important of these I was to discover one day when I was passing the school stage. This was an area that backed off the canteen and was opened only for the annual school concert. It was accessed by a door that was usually locked unless one of the teachers, Miss Ní Chinnéide, was practising, as she was often heard to do during the lunch break.

I was on my way to Ní Chinnéide's classroom when I heard the sound of the piano. Worried about an upcoming oral Irish exam, I was seeking advice. I knocked at the stage door but there was no answer. When I eased the door open I found the area in darkness but the music went on. I closed the door, stood still and felt the melody vibrate up through the floorboards. Ní Chinnéide was good – very good. I'd heard her play before when the school put on musicals, but not like this. The melody skipped and swayed and completely absorbed me. I was late for chemistry class, really late, but I couldn't tear myself away.

It stopped abruptly, jolting me from my hypnotic state.

'Miss?'

Silence and then a scuffle in the darkness. Panic beat in my chest, a small bird seeking escape.

'Is someone there?'

A foolish question – there wasn't a phantom pianist who had evaporated when the music ceased. I felt near the door for the light switch, but before I could locate it someone grabbed me and spun me round. I hollered and fought the hand on my shoulder.

'Sssh, quiet, someone will hear you'.

Maybe that's why his voice was so distinctive to me, because I'd heard it first in the dark. Well, that wasn't entirely true. I'd heard him speak in class, of course, but it was the first time he'd spoken to me.

'Donal?'

'Sssh'.

An arm guiding me towards the door and then the sound of him fumbling for the handle. I squinted at the rectangle of light as he eased the door open and then cautiously poked his head into the corridor. He was outside in one swift movement pulling me with him.

'Chemistry ...'

He shrugged. 'Can't go in now, can we? Maguire'd have a fit'. Eyes casing the corridor. I stood, uncertain which way to turn, until they fixed on me, huge behind black-rimmed glasses. 'You coming or what?' And it was that abrupt invitation that sealed the friendship between us.

We exited the school through a gap in the railing. Donal stopped to peel off his school jumper and tied it around his waist. I noticed his hands as he did it, large, cumbersome – the knuckles of his fingers wide.

'Where did you learn to play like that?' I asked.

He shrugged. 'We had a piano at home. This woman used to come round twice a week to give me lessons'.

I almost had to trot to keep up with his long stride. 'I've never heard anyone play so well ... I mean, I've heard Miss Ní Chinnéide, but you ... you're really good. Did she give you permission to practise there?'

Donal looked down at me and grinned. I'd never seen him smile before. It was like someone had switched on a bulb, not one of those energy-saver things, but blinding, incandescent. 'Why do you think I was sitting in there in the dark?' he said.

That afternoon was the first of many after-school trips to Donal's house. He lived in a council estate like mine with his parents, Remy, his younger brother and Rosco, a German shepherd that put his paws on my shoulders and his muzzle to my face terrifying me that first afternoon.

One of the first things I looked for in the house was the piano, but there was none. Donal said it had been sold with the house in Killiney. Everything had been sold, except Rosco. He fondled the big dog's ears as it sat princely by his side. Killiney. I'd only been out that way once on a picnic. My mother had taken us into town and we got the Dart out to Killiney beach. It had felt like the journey to middle earth from our west Dublin suburb. Mam told us that all the rich people lived there – that Elton John had considered buying one of those big white houses that looked down on the bay.

'Was it beautiful, the house?' I asked Donal. He was going through a pile of vinyl – carefully extracting David Bowie's *Spiders from Mars* album from its sleeve when he looked up.

'Would you like to see it?' he said. I nodded and we decided that at the weekend, me, him and Rosco would take the Dart out to see the house where they had lived.

The bus driver looked at us like we'd no savvy.

'You can't take that thing on the bus', he said.

Rosco barked and Donal shushed him, clamping his hand round his muzzle.

'He's a guide dog in training', he said. 'He won't be any trouble. If he is you can tell us to get off'.

The man hmmphed, not believing a word, but he let us on and we stood, keeping Rosco on a tight lead as the bus rattled into the city centre.

On the Dart we got funny looks, wary looks. Passengers were afraid of Rosco who eyed them with curiosity, nose working at each new scent. When he became too interested in a newcomer or their shopping bag Donal offered him a treat from his pocket, but Rosco crunched, once, twice and it was gone and he was back again on the scent of something. Still, nobody told us to get off and so we arrived in Killiney in the early afternoon – my stomach almost caving for the want of the sandwiches I'd made that morning, wrapped in tinfoil in my backpack.

As soon as we got off the train Rosco tugged at the lead. He smelt the salty brine. Did he think he had come home, I wondered, to the big house in Killiney?

'You can't really see it from the road', Donal told me. 'We have to go down to the beach and look back up at it'.

We followed a set of steps down to the beach. It was low tide but there was a wind and a couple of guys were out in the bay with surfboards. It reminded me of one of those Australian soaps, except not as warm, so I tried to button my skimpy denim jacket against the wind and tug the hair that was blowing in my face at the same time. Rosco ran happily in front, smelling seaweed and sea life washed up on the strand, oblivious to us.

'That's it. Do you see? That terracotta house? Can't see much of it, I suppose, from here'. Donal pointed upwards and I shaded my eyes with one hand and followed his pointing finger. The house was high up on the road we'd descended from, down all those steps. There was a garden too, palm trees swaying behind the rocky wall at what I imagined to be the back of the bungalow.

'Why did you move?' I asked.

We were walking now, leaving the house behind. There were families on the beach, small children running around, fascinated and terrified of the water. They ran to the edge and squealed when a small wave washed over their feet.

Donal looked serious now. 'The old man drank the roof from over our heads. He had his own business, the house, everything. The business got into trouble and he remortgaged the house to try to dig it out – but the problem wasn't business, it was him – pissing it all away. Now, he's supposedly on the dry'. Donal grunted at this, disbelieving. 'It's only a matter of time, of course, and then I'll go home to find my mother crying, things smashed up, people'. Donal picked up a bit of stick and threw it for the dog, vehemently. 'I swear, I'll never drink – not when I see what it's done to him, to all of us'.

'How old is your brother?'

'Twelve'.

'I never see him around the house'.

'Remy has Aspergers. He doesn't really mix with other kids. He likes numbers and things, facts – he has an uncanny ability to memorise them. Mam has a set routine for him, anything that goes against it really upsets him, like the old man's drinking ... but then that would upset anyone'.

I was distracted by the closeness of Donal's hand which occasionally brushed mine. I itched to take it, to feel his big fingers close round mine – but I didn't dare.

'My parents separated when I was three', I said.

'Yeah?' He stopped walking to take off his glasses, lifting the corner of his t-shirt to clean the lenses. His eyes were the deepest blue, lashes dark as night. He'd already started shaving and a few black hairs stippled his jaw where he'd missed them with the razor. 'What happened?'

I turned my gaze to the moiling sea. 'Same thing – drink. My mother didn't want me growing up in that environment, so she got him out. I don't remember much about him'.

'Where is he now?'

'Dead – hit by a car walking in the middle of the N81 at three in the morning'.

'Jesus'.

'Yeah, I suppose it's tragic. But it didn't affect me, not really, he may as well have been a stranger'.

Rosco had stopped ahead, he waited now for us to catch him up, he'd chewed the stick into pieces. Donal kneeled to pet him. The dog put his paws against his chest making him lose his balance and the two of them tumbled onto the sand.

I met Remy a few days after that. One of the bedroom doors was ajar. Passing it on my way to the bathroom, I heard a voice. 'A million earths can fit inside the sun'. I paused in the landing, not sure whether he was talking to me or if maybe there was someone in his room. When I looked up he was sitting on the edge of the bed, a book in his hand, looking directly at me. He bore a strong resemblance to Donal. I wasn't sure whether I should go in or not. I stopped at the door and looked in. 'You must be Remy'.

'Neutron stars can spin at a rate of six hundred rotations per second'.

'Wow, I didn't know that. What are you reading?'

Slowly, I entered the room. Remy didn't look up. He showed me a picture – a vast sky filled with millions of tiny blue and orange dots, of cloudy masses of constellations. I sat on the bed and peered at it. Remy didn't react.

'Space is completely silent. There's no medium for sound waves to travel through'. He didn't look at me when he said it, and I wondered if Remy liked the thought of living in a silent, uninhabited space where he wasn't obliged to communicate with anyone.

I looked around the room. I could see the outline of millions of stars on Remy's ceiling. In the night he must lie there and stare up at his own mini-galaxies. In daylight, the glow was subdued, almost non-existent. There were some posters on the walls – one of Mars, another of Pluto. A glass paper-weight sat on the small desk next to Remy's bed. I picked it up, saw my own face in the reflection and beneath it sky and endless stars.

Donal was surprised to find me perched on the bed next to his brother, not exactly having a conversation, but invited temporarily into his closed universe.

'He doesn't usually talk to anyone', Donal told me. 'Well, to us, of course, but not to strangers. He must have decided you're different'. He smiled and I took that 'different' as the highest compliment I'd ever been paid.

Donal passed me a note one day in maths class. The lightbulb was on – more than that he was excited to the extent that he couldn't still his limbs, one foot kept tapping as though to a tune that only he could hear, his movements causing the table to tremor under my copybook. He'd seen a keyboard in a charity shop and he was cutting class to go there and try to bargain with the assistant. 'Not a piano', he'd written, 'but still'. He joked that he was going electric, like Bob Dylan. 'Come over later', he told me, before racing out of class, 'with any luck, I'll have it'.

As soon as school had finished, I gathered my books and left. It was one of those hot, dull days of early summer. I exited through the gap in the railing and followed the path across the field that I'd got used to taking during the three months of our friendship. I must have been halfway across the field when I saw the blue lights. It was at the point where Donal's house usually came into view. I thought at first that Donal's heavily-pregnant neighbour must have finally gone into labour, but then I saw the police cars – three of them, with an ambulance parked outside the house, Donal's house, and I began to run.

My lungs were burning by the time I got to the start of the block of houses. A crowd had gathered on the road and the police were telling them to stay back, that the area was a crime scene. I grabbed someone's arm and asked them what was happening, but the neighbour shrugged and said no one knew. I fought my way through the crowd opposite the house and went up to a garda.

'What's going on?'

'If you can just stay back, please', she said.

'I'm a friend of the family. Is ... is someone hurt?'

'There's been a domestic', she said. Jesus. I thought of Donal's words – only a matter of time, he'd said, until something, someone. His father must have started drinking again, but who was it he had hurt – Donal's mother, or Remy maybe? But where was Donal? He should have been home by now. He'd left school a couple of hours before. There was no way he was still haggling with the assistant over the keyboard.

And then I saw him, Donal. There was a surge of noise, muttering, neighbours elbowing each other, faces jostling to get a better look. Donal was being led from the house, hands behind his back – a garda on either side of him. His mother appeared behind him, crying, clawing at him, trying to pull him back. 'No, no, he didn't do it. Please'. Donal looked calm. His blue eyes looked up for a moment, scanned the crowd.

'Donie!' My voice a strangled roar as I fought my way to the front. A policeman blocked my way and I just glimpsed past him to see Donal loaded into the back of one of the patrol cars – his head forcefully ducked like in the movies – and in the background, Remy being led away, head lowered, a strange woman whooshing him along, propelling him towards a parked car.

It was only through the papers that I discovered that Donal's father had been killed – struck on the back of the head by a blunt object. His mother had tried to take the blame, but they knew it wasn't her and they'd already had a confession from Donal.

My mother wouldn't hear of me going to visit Donal in the young offenders' institution. She wasn't completely unsympathetic though, she stroked my hair and said she knew how I felt about Donal and that maybe it wasn't the poor lad's fault what happened. She suggested that I write a letter, she even offered to go with me to his mother's house so I could give it to her to pass on. It was more out of a macabre curiosity to meet the McMahons and see the place for herself, I thought, but we went anyway – a month after Donal had been taken away.

It was hard not to imagine where it had happened. I found myself looking for blood stains on the carpet – for evidence that the father had fallen and lain prostrate until the ambulance had arrived. My mother sympathised, said that I'd been very fond of Donal, that we were great pals at school. Then they got talking of other things and I excused myself to go upstairs to the bathroom.

The door to Remy's room was closed. I knocked gently and opened it. He looked up and then lowered his eyes again to the book he was reading.

'The human brain ceases activity ten seconds after death'.

I didn't say anything, but turned my head a fraction to see his face.

'The body stays warm for up to twelve hours'.

I didn't ask Remy how he knew this – the book that lay in his lap had nothing to do with science. Maybe they'd discussed it at school. I didn't take science class. My friend's sister had told me how they'd had to dissect a cow's eyeball and that was it for me.

Remy straightened and rubbed his eyes. My heart was doing flip-flops with anxiety. I wanted to slow it down, to breathe normally again, but I had to hear it. I had to wait.

'The paperweight weighs six hundred and twenty-two grams', he said.

I looked round to where the paperweight lay on Remy's desk, but it was gone. I pictured it shattered, tiny specks of blood staining the stars red, an implosion of the cosmos. Remy turned to look at me. 'When is Donal coming home?' he said.

I don't know if Donal ever got my letter. He didn't write back – or if he did his answer never got to me. Maybe my mother had intercepted it. She was relieved, I'm sure, when I threw myself into studying for my Leaving Certificate, then I got a place in UCD studying English and met someone on the course.

Donal. I'd heard that his mother died only two years after he was sent away. Nobody told me at the time, I imagined they'd allowed him to go to the funeral. I wondered if he'd looked for me there. Or if maybe he'd forgotten me entirely. I had no idea what had happened to Remy after that.

Donie Mac. Did he think that I'd dissed him, purposefully failed to recognize him back there in the lane? Christ. The train hurtled on. At every station, I thought about getting off, of going back to see if it was really him. And what if it was? What if it really was Donie? Ironically, it was that that stopped me. What would I say to him now after all that time?

It was two days before I saw him again. I saw the movement in the shadows as he shifted position, my heels clicking a warning in the laneway.

'Spare change ...'

I stopped to look at him. Blue eyes huge behind black-framed glasses – looking not at me, but past me – and it was then that I realised it wasn't Donal, but Remy. His eyes clicked into focus when I said his name.

'It's Tara, remember? Donal's friend, Tara'.

'Tara', he repeated. Then he looked away.

'What are you doing here?' I asked him.

'Dead', he said. 'They're all dead'. He looked down the lane past me. I thought he was going to ask the next passer-by to spare some change, but he didn't.

'Not Donal?'

'Donal. Donal didn't come home'. Remy paused. 'Sixteen people go missing every day. Nobody ever finds them'.

'Missing? No Remy, Donal's not missing. But you – have you no place to go?'

He pointed in the direction of the seafront. I walked with him, found that he'd been sleeping in a wind shelter in front of the promenade. He pointed out to sea – eyes squinting into the light.

'There are at least twenty-eight types of gull in North America', he said. And without turning his gaze from the water, 'Will you help to find Donal?'

'Yes, Remy', I said, raising my hand but then letting it drop again to my side. 'I'll help. I'll help you to find Donal'.

What Happened at the Clarkes'

It wouldn't have happened if Miranda had allowed me to book us into a hotel as I'd wanted. She was twenty-two and still unable to extricate herself from the shadow of her parents' pious beliefs. In truth, Miranda had flouted those beliefs months before when she'd persuaded me to sleep with her.

Miranda. Sweet, petulant Miranda. I first spotted her, or I should say she spotted me, when we both signed up for a creative writing class at a literary festival. She was a budding short story writer, I a would-be poet, who seduced her, she claimed, with words. There'd been a mix-up between the festival organisers and the course facilitator – my work had got lost in transit. I was explaining that I'd been told to send the work directly to the university where the facilitator worked when a girl interjected with a sudden 'yeah, yeah, yeah' from across the room.

Miranda. Seated directly opposite me, fedora perched on the back of her head, long blonde hair framing her face, she twirled her pen and met my look of annoyance with a wide smile that disarmed me. Over coffee at the break, she asked what my mystery manuscript had been about. She was clever, Miranda, but totally unpretentious. The bohemian look she wore was her – not some arty guise designed for notice. It was only in the company of her parents that Miranda reverted to a somewhat more toned-down version of herself. As though she didn't want to sully the pristine image they had of her.

They were well-off, the Clarkes. Not mega-rich, but they had a nice house on a couple of acres in County Wicklow. We'd been going out about four months when Miranda announced that her parents were throwing a bash for her grandmother's 70th. There was to be a marquee, live music, her brother, Kris, was coming home from London for the weekend. It would be an ideal time to meet the family.

I imagined Miranda would be delighted at my suggestion of booking into a spa hotel. But she said her parents had invited us to stay for the weekend; that it would be an insult to refuse. And so it was settled.

Saturday came. Miranda picked me up at midday in her little red Beatle and we headed out the N11. She was excited, said she'd had a text from Kris who'd got in from London the night before. Miranda got that look about her when she talked about Kris, the same look she got when she talked about books or music – or anything that impressed her. Her face blazed with enthusiasm.

Kris was an actor, she said. He'd once played Brick in *Cat on a Hot Tin Roof* and the local papers had raved about it. The previous year he'd gone to London to audition for movies – he'd got a few walk-on parts, but she was sure it wouldn't be long before he was cast in a more significant role. Kris, she said, had presence.

I watched Miranda as she talked, hands gripping the wheel, cheeks tinged pink from the wind that rocketed through the open windows. The Glen of the Downs flashed past as her words infused the air with inexorable vigour. She laughed when a sudden gust caught her fedora and propelled it onto the back seat – and her hair, suddenly freed, danced round her in abandon. That's the image I retain of Miranda. Even after all that happened.

Miranda's mood was still buoyant as we turned into the long gravel drive that led to her parents' house. Two other cars were parked outside, a black Mercedes and a sleek silver coupe. Miranda switched off the ignition and turned towards me, hand on my leg.

'I should've mentioned, you'll have to share Kris's room. My parents are a bit, you know, old-fashioned like that'.

'No worries, that's ok'. I smiled, not altogether surprised by Miranda's revelation. In those days my parents would have been reticent if I'd brought a girl home to stay.

She leaned in and nibbled my bottom lip – then my top, her hand straying from my knee. 'Of course that doesn't mean we can't get up to anything. There'll be plenty of distractions with the party'. Miranda's hot breath fanned my ear. She nuzzled my neck, then sat upright with a 'now's the moment' look. 'Come on, they'll be around the back'.

She led me through an archway between the house and the garage. At the end of a magnificent lawn surrounded by trees a marquee was being erected. Two men were busy rolling up the entrance door and securing it. As we crossed the lawn a woman emerged from the house. She raised a hand and smiled and I knew before Miranda told me that it was her mother.

'You must be Liam. Miranda's told us all about you. Of course, I don't believe the half of it. She's a terrible fantasist'. Miranda's mother winked and led us into a long, cool kitchen where she'd prepared a cold lunch for us. Miranda had coloured slightly, I wasn't sure if it was from her mother's remark or the anticipation of seeing her brother.

'Where's Kris?' Miranda asked, crossing to the window and looking towards the marquee. Her mother busied herself removing cellophane from the salad dishes. 'Knowing Kris, he's wherever the work isn't', she said. Miranda went out to the hall and shouted up the stairs for her brother.

'So Liam, I hear you met Miranda at a writing class. What do you write, stories?'

'Poetry mostly, I'm trying to get into writing short stories. Not sure I have a talent for it yet, not like Miranda'.

'Miranda has quite the fertile imagination. I can't say I ever really got it myself. I suppose it's all that reading. It always seemed such a waste of time to me. Kris is the same, except with him it's films. I thought he'd grow out of it …'

'Grow out of what?'

We turned to see a tall, young man in the doorway – hands dug deep in khaki trousers. Everything about Kris was dark – hair, skin, even his countenance. But his eyes were an almost transparent green. I guessed it was Miranda's description of his playing Brick that had made me think he'd be blonde like her. But the person in the doorway was much more a brooding Heathcliff than a Paul Newman.

'Play-acting', his mother said. 'You'll tire of it some day'.

Kris entered the room. 'Nothing wrong with a little fantasy, is there?' He extended his hand. 'Liam, I take it?' I shook the hand he offered, noticing how my skin looked almost translucent next to his.

Just then Miranda returned – 'Why Master Clarke, I do declare', she said, her accent every bit the Southern belle. She tipped her fedora and grinned. When she put her arms round her brother's neck, he embraced her, lifting her clear with one arm. Their mother looked at me and shook her head. Blood surged, setting my cheeks aflame.

'Liam, you may as well put your stuff in Kris's room', Miranda said, taking the hat from her head and placing it on her brother's. She took me by the arm and followed Kris up the stairs.

Kris's room had wall-to-wall DVDs. Many of them were dramas; several versions of Shakespeare's comedies, along with a whole collection of Tennessee Williams' plays. I didn't think he'd grow out of his tendency towards make-believe any time soon. Miranda flung herself on her brother's bed, the only one in the room, I noted, as I looked for a place to put my bag.

'Any auditions lately?' Miranda asked.

'A few, nothing worth talking about'. Kris picked up a dart and flung it at a board, narrowly missing a bull's eye. 'What time's the party kicking off?'

'We said eight. So Dad'll be bringing Nana Lena across before that. Are you going to give us a performance? Wait till you hear Kris sing', she said, turning to me. Miranda's admiration for her brother was not lacking foundation. Kris had more talent than anyone I'd met.

By eight, the guests had started to arrive. Miranda introduced me to cousins, and to her grandmother, who at 70, reminded me of a still glamorous Sophia Loren. The former actress took my hands in hers and kissed my cheek.

'You didn't say how handsome he was, Mira'.

Miranda stretched to kiss her grandmother's cheek. 'Lena charms all the men'.

My face burned for a second time and when I looked beyond Miranda, Kris raised an eyebrow and smiled. It was evident that Nana Lena was a major influence on both her grandchildren.

Miranda flitted all evening between the guests, a sprite in a flame-coloured dress, blonde hair curled to her shoulders in the absence of the fedora. When darkness came we walked the garden. Coloured lights had been strung along the path, lending the grounds a carnivalesque atmosphere. Miranda, hand through my arm, talked about her mother and her turbulent relationship with Nana Lena.

'Mom didn't like us spending too much time around her, but we were just mad about her'. She smiled. 'I'm sure you've seen that. Lena was always exotic. Not like a grandmother, maybe more a fairy grandmother. Kris and me were convinced she could do magic. It kills mom that we both took after her. She'd like us to be bankers or solicitors or something, not arty layabouts as she likes to say'.

Miranda sat on a swing seat just in view of the marquee and I sat next to her. She leaned in and kissed me. 'Mom has her reasons. Lena wasn't your conventional mother. She was always off somewhere, following some whim or other and mom and her brothers were left very much to themselves. Granddad was an engineer in the Air Corps. He was crazy about Lena – and he was strict with the kids where Lena wasn't, but I think mom appreciated that. It showed he cared. I don't remember Granddad, he died not long after I was born'.

Miranda stopped. Voices and laughter drifted from the marquee amplified in the still night air. She nuzzled my shoulder. We sat like that for a time until the twang of a guitar sounded in the darkness and sparked Miranda into motion. 'Sounds like the band's warming up, let's go inside'. She stood, took my hands and attempted to pull me to my feet. I resisted and she pushed against my hands and grinned. 'What's the matter, Massah, don't ya wanna dance?'

I kissed the fingers of her right hand. 'I think I'll just sit a while'.

She looked at me and then in a sing-song voice said, 'do I feel the muse a-coming?' I nodded, and she brushed my lips with hers. 'Right-o, I'll see you inside'.

I watched Miranda cross the lawn and heard her laughter as she stopped to talk to a group by the entrance. The band had started, a jazzy number that drifted from the confines of the tent and stole into the night. I breathed deep and tried to still a feeling of unease that had begun to claw at my insides, but it refused to be mollified. It had started back at the house – a stirring of a kind that I'd denied once, a year before I'd met Miranda. But the unacknowledged has a way of returning.

Slowly, I made my way towards the marquee. One of Miranda's cousins raised her wine glass, 'You're just in time to hear Kris play'. I entered, the girl close behind me, and scanned the tent for Miranda. She was in deep conversation with a guy who had tattoos wound the length of each arm. He looked rapt by whatever story Miranda was telling. But then most people were. Her words drew people in.

On the stage Kris was adjusting a guitar, Miranda's fedora on his head. He played with the tuning pegs before plucking a few strings. The sound reverberated in my skull or maybe it was the wine I'd drunk too quickly. I wasn't accustomed then to anything stronger than the occasional beer. Kris said something into a mic, which I didn't quite catch and Miranda's tattooed friend took his place behind the drum-kit. Miranda, having lost her audience, came over. 'Was wondering where you were. I thought you'd gone to scribble down whatever the muse brought'.

I shook my head. 'To be honest, I've an awful headache'.

'Wait till you hear Kris. He's brilliant'. She was staring at the stage, a glass in her hand. I wasn't sure she'd even heard me.

Kris *was* brilliant. Miranda was right about that. His voice, powerful yet restrained, resonated, transfixing us both. He sang *Georgia on My Mind,* one of her grandmother's favourites Miranda told me, and we watched as one of the men took Lena's hand and brought her onto the dance floor. Miranda nudged me, 'Isn't she beautiful?' I smiled, eyes fixed on the stage and gulped the last of my wine.

The evening moved on, the knot unwinding with each refill of my glass. The musicians finished, but the singing didn't stop. A guitar was passed round and various family members were called on to sing. Others weren't, but sang anyway. Kris had had as much to drink as the rest of us, it seemed. He'd lost the brooding look and entertained us with impersonations so good that he had Miranda wiping her eyes, eyeliner smudged down her cheeks.

In the early hours, we said goodbye to the last of the clan. Nana Lena had long since retired, as had Miranda's parents and some of the younger cousins had pitched tents in the yard. Shouts and muffled laughter came from within as we passed; the three of us with arms flung drunkenly round each other.

'Liam, you didn't sing tonight', Kris said.

'I don't know the words of anything, just a few half songs'.

He stumbled and tightened his arm round my neck almost bringing the three of us down. 'What do you like?'

'I don't know, a lot of old stuff, Bowie, The Stones, The Doors'.

'Ok, you've got to know this one. Everyone knows this one'. He started singing, 'You know that it would be untrue, you know that I would be a liar …' Miranda and I joined in, but she didn't know the second verse and Kris and I kept going. He pointed his free hand at me, his face close to mine as we negotiated the lyrics. He placed the fedora on my head. Miranda had begun dancing, lifting the ends of her flame-coloured dress and flipping it from side to side, flamenco-style. Her hair fell in her eyes as she swayed across the lawn a few steps in front of us. She turned and put a finger to her lips as we neared the house.

'Ssh, we'll wake the conformists'.

'The what?'

Kris grinned. 'That's what she calls the folks, we have to curb it a bit around them ... especially with mum. She already thinks we're too much like Lena'.

Miranda stopped at the door, smoothened her dress, mock-respectably. Kris still had his arm around my shoulder.

Miranda led the way upstairs. In the landing she stopped to kiss us both goodnight. She reached up, arms round my neck and kissed me lightly on the lips. Then she did the same with her brother. She winked, put her finger to her lips again and went into her room, while I followed Kris to his.

In darkness, I heard him shut the door behind us. He knocked against the bedside locker and the lamp rocked back and forth until he stilled it and brought the room to life. I sat on the edge of the bed to take off my shoes.

'That was some party', Kris stretched, pulled his t-shirt over his head and threw it in a corner. I laughed and nodded, self-conscious now we were alone. I looked away as he unbuckled his jeans and stepped out of them.

'Miranda's great. She was so excited about seeing you. It was all she talked about the last few days'.

Kris smiled and I tried to ignore his eyes on me as, awkwardly, I undressed. 'That kid would do anything for me', he said. He climbed beneath the covers, pulled his pillow down and lay with one arm crooked under his head.

'You ever tried acting, Liam?'

'No, never'. I stared at the ceiling, avoiding his eyes. 'But I really admire people who do. I'd never be able to remember the lines …'

'It's not so hard. You just become someone else … think their thoughts, be as they are'.

He'd left the light on. I turned away from him, away from the heat of his body. The knot had wound itself round my gut again and I felt too sober.

'I suppose it's not too different from writing, Liam, getting inside other people's minds, being something you're not'.

I heard him remove his hand from under his head, then felt it on my shoulder, on the back of my neck. I tensed and in protest turned slightly towards him.

'Ssh, relax', he said. 'It's easy'.

He was saying things close to my ear when I heard the door being eased open. A shaft of dim light crept into the darkened room and fell across our bodies. Either he didn't see or chose to ignore it, but Kris continued to move against me, hands on my shoulders, as I turned my head slightly to the side and heard rather than saw the door close again.

'Miranda'.

'Ssh'.

He hushed her name on my lips – and I knew why it was that I'd been brought to this place, why Miranda had turned down my offer of the hotel in the Wicklow hills. After that night I vowed never to see either of the Clarkes again.

Shadows

I fumble in darkness, search for the light switch and close my eyes until the flickering fades to a steady light.

'You're late'. Adam sits in an armchair in the corner, the remote control in his lap. His clothes are dishevelled.

'We went for a drink afterwards'.

'Afterwards what?' he says.

'After the workshop', I say. 'You know I had class tonight'.

I fill the kettle. He mumbles something, his words drowned by the surge from the tap. I push in the plug and flick the switch. 'What did you say?' I ask.

'I said I didn't know, you never told me. You never – asked me'.

His words are slurred. I do not answer. I know better than to answer. It would only go on for the night. I take two mugs from the stand on the sink and rinse them beneath the hot tap.

Adam rises. I see his reflection in the windowpane. He sways slightly and comes towards me. I busy myself spooning coffee from a container.

'Is this what he teaches you?' He puts an arm around my waist. His grip is iron. He tries to twist me towards him, lead me in the steps of a drunken waltz.

'Stop messing about, Adam'.

'Messing about, is that what I'm doing? Is that what he does?'

His breath stinks of beer, his fingers biting into my flesh. I will not rise to his bait. I turn to face him. 'Sit down and I'll bring you your coffee'.

'Yes, ma'am'. He raises his hand in mock salute, releases me and half-stumbles back to his chair. I grip the sink with both hands, my legs weak. The smell lingers, crudely familiar. I am a child again, cowering in the hallway, watching the figure outside.

The shadow moved again, shifted across the amber glass. I squatted on the third step of the stairs, my legs cramped in position. The thud of the knocker sounded once more. Louder this time, more impatient.

'Come on, let me in'.

My mother drew back as though he may suddenly reach through the door. She stood immobile, one foot balanced on the rung of the tall stool, the burnt-out light bulb in one hand as she raised the other to her lips.

I prayed that he would not look through the letterbox. That he would not see me cowering, head between my knees trying to disappear. The pattern on the carpet blurred, spirals melting together. I could smell the dust, see the dog hairs stuck between the ridges. There was silence. Then I heard his footsteps clatter on the tarmac.

The squeak as the garden gate was closed. My mother moved closer to the spy hole.

'It's ok, he's gone'. She ran a hand through her hair. 'It's ok'.

She said it more to herself than to me. I stood up, the backs of my knees aching, my knuckles cramped from gripping the banister so tight. My mother took the stool and carried it back into the kitchen. She wrapped the bulb in newspaper and put it in the bin. Her hands were shaking.

'Do you think he'll come back?'

'We won't be here if he does', she said.

I ease the remote control from his fingers. His head falls to one side, rests upon his chest. He stirs. His eyes flicker in sleep. I switch the television off. His snores invade the silence; sound consecutively abreast the ticking of the clock. I will go to bed, leave him be in the hope that he is out for the night.

Tiredness arrests me, my body sags and my feet drag upon the steps. I straighten the blanket in the empty cot, trail my fingers along its fleecy softness. Molly's bear lies against the bars, lonesome. She'll miss him tonight. I struggle out of my clothing, lay them on the chair for the morning. In the morning, I will collect her. I fumble for the clock and set it to alarm before he rises.

Time passes. With my eyes half-open I watch the bedroom door, listen for his foot upon the stairs. In darkness I watch as the lights of a passing car cross and re-cross the walls. And I feel as though I've done it all before.

I followed my mother up the stairs, watched as she threw things into a carrier bag. Clean underwear, toothbrushes, comb. She took a clean pair of jeans from the hot press and told me to put them on. My room was dark. I reversed the venetian blind so that the streetlight filtered through the slats and was mirrored on the far wall. We dared not turn on the light. He might still have been out there and saw the sign of life. I raised my arms, pulled my pyjama jacket over my head. My mother threw me a clean sweater from beyond the hot press door. I heard the swish as she closed it and her footsteps on the stairs. I struggled to get my head through the opening. I didn't like to be alone in the dark.

Molly sits on the floor, playing with her building bricks. She gurgles when she sees me, stretches out her arms. 'Mama'. I swing her up and balance her on my hip. She smells of sweet baby smells, of baby talc. Her skin is soft.

'You're early', my mother says.

'I thought we might do something. Maybe go for a drive?'

Molly presses her hands against my face. Her fingers are sticky. She pulls at my nose and laughs.

'That would be nice'. Her face seems to light. 'Where will we go?'

'Anywhere', I say. I strap Molly into the baby chair. She waves her hands about and giggles. My mother is all busy. I feel guilty, she thinks that much of getting out. She emerges, handbag bulging. She might have stepped from the pages of some middle-aged *Vogue*. She hasn't done too badly on her own.

I take her out to Wicklow, through Hollywood and up the gap. Clumps of heather blaze on the mountainside. The sun transforms the scorched earth. Sometimes I feel her eyes upon me. I keep mine on the road, watchful of the stray sheep and wary of my stray thoughts.

We arrive in Laragh. The village is alive with tourists, cameras slung round their necks, tanned legs revealed in khaki shorts.

'I always loved this place', my mother says. 'Do you remember I used to bring you here in the old Fiat?'

'I remember the night it broke down', I say.

She laughs. 'Still it was a good old car'.

The sign outside the dormer cottage reads *May's Tea-rooms,* the menu written in chalk on a board. I pull up against the low wall. My mother steps out, takes Molly and heads for a table in the sun. I go inside and order. When I come out they are laughing. Molly points at a shaggy dog, its leg cocked against a tree. 'Dirty doggy', my mother says.

'Doggy, doggy', Molly says, delighted with the new word. She wriggles on my mother's lap.

I take her and swing her high in the air.

'You'll kill that child', my mother says. She shakes her head.

I sit down, breathe in the scent of summer. In this place I could almost forget. But I can't, can I? Not when I have to go home again, to God-knows-what tonight.

'How was your class last night?' My mother is watching me.

'Good', I say, 'it was good'.

I watch as she spreads a dollop of strawberry jam on a hot scone. Her hand is steady. The woman from the cottage crosses the grass to where a group of weary hikers sit slumped at a table in the shade, their haversacks thrown on the ground at their feet. Molly reaches forward, throws her beaker on the ground. Milk dribbles into the grass. I clasp her on my lap and lean down to pick it up. The peace is shattered by the thunder of a motorcycle – several motorcycles. They ride in convoy across the bridge and pull up outside Lynham's pub. I sit back and watch them talk and laugh. One of them reminds me of a boy I knew in school. Long before I met Adam.

'I could take Molly for a few days. If you're tired ... if you need some time ...'

'I'm fine', I say. 'Fine'.

My mother gives me that look. The look that she used to give me when I was younger and she knew that I wasn't telling the truth. She nods and sips her tea. Her eyes are a clear green as she stares into the distance, to some place I cannot follow. More than ever now I wish that we'd spoken about it. It might make it easier. I might be able to say, 'Mother, I don't know what to do', but I can't because I, like her, have my damned pride. I need to know whether she ever looked back? Whether what she did was right for her? But our past is like another life. A life that is, by some unspoken agreement, never alluded to.

'Laura, we need to talk'.

The words are sharp, clear and for a moment leave me silent.

She folds and unfolds her hands. Her eyes do not leave my face. She is asking me to tell her. Leaving it open after all this time, because through love she senses my desperation.

We opened the hall door, and cautiously stepped outside, but there was no sign of the shadow. My mother unlocked the car doors and threw the bags into the back, then she stooped beneath the steering wheel, pulled a lever and the bonnet opened with a pop. She got out and took the blanket off the engine, dropped the bonnet shut.

'Now, get ready to step in when I tell you'. She turned the key in the ignition, the car spluttered, but did not start. She tried it again, this time it coughed into life. She pumped the accelerator and smoke belched from the exhaust.

'Now, press that pedal if you think it's going to stop. Don't let it cut out'. She got out and I sat into the driver's seat.

She slammed the door and I watched as she jumped over the garden wall that separated us from the neighbours. She rang the bell and waited on the doorstep, looked up and down the road. It was freezing in the car, the heater didn't work. I hoped that she wouldn't be long. I was afraid that he would come back, that he might appear from behind one of the bushes that rustled in the wind. I pressed the pedal and tried to block out the noise and the silence.

'Laura. Will you open the goddamn door?'

The shadow moves, shifts beyond the frosted glass. I hear the scraping of his key against the lock, the rattle as he drops the bundle to the ground.

'Fucking lock', he says.

I cradle Molly in my arms. Somehow she sleeps through the noise. He swears again, bangs the porch door closed. I stand in silence. My eyes adjust to the darkness, the shape of his boots beneath the stairs. Molly breathes easy against my breast. I listen to his footsteps on the tarmac as they fade into the night.

WHY, MOLLY?

Molly stands in the doorway, portfolio clutched beneath one arm and watches Jake clear the snow from the driveway. Head bowed in concentration, he hasn't seen her come out of the house. The shovel scrapes on the tarmac and he tosses another pile of dirty snow onto the lawn. Molly wishes he wouldn't do that. She loves the first snow, how its brilliance transforms the grey apathy of winter.

'I'm going', she says. Jake looks up at the sound of her voice. In one red-gloved hand she raises the portfolio and waves it at him.

He lowers the shovel and looks at the sky. 'Are you sure it's going ahead?'

Molly nods. 'I rang the centre this afternoon'. She buttons up her coat, fingers clumsy in her gloves. On her head a matching red beret he bought her at Christmas. Stray snowflakes drift from a laden sky, they catch and melt in her long brown hair. Jake crosses the now-clear driveway, shovel in hand.

'What time will I pick you up?' he says.

'There's no need – besides, it's safer walking'.

He nods, looks at the car parked on the road. That afternoon he'd scraped the snow from the windscreen. Then he'd turned the engine on and left it running. He didn't want the block to crack, he said.

Molly arrives at the arts centre fifteen minutes before the class is to start. The windows have been blacked out and it looks as though it is closed, but when she tries the door it gives. She steps into the heat. It's a small room that can fit seven or eight artists at most. Already some of them have arrived. They clamber for a good position to set their easels up, big bulky frames from behind which they'll peer at the model. In the centre of the room is a mattress covered by a plain white sheet.

Molly stamps the snow from her boots and plucks off her red gloves. She's examining the layout of the room when a man comes out a door marked 'Staff Only'.

'First night? Just grab an easel from the corner and set up. We'll be starting …'

'I'm the model', Molly interrupts.

'Ah, of course. In that case, come this way. I'm Jim'. His handshake is firm. He leads Molly through the door from which he entered. A curtained space in the corner of the room acts as a makeshift cubicle. He tells her she can change and come out when she's done. Unlike the studio, the room is cold – Molly takes off her backpack and unpacks her slippers and robe. Carefully she puts her portfolio into the bag, sketchpad, charcoals, things she has no use for other than to deceive her husband.

She shivers as she undresses – feet bare on the cold tiled floor. In the studio, noise of easels being set up, the hum of friendly banter among the artists. Suddenly she is nervous. She stands before the mirror and appraises herself in the glass. Long legs – model's legs – he used to say, between them a nest of dark hair. Breasts, small and rounded. She slips on the dressing gown and enters the studio.

Jim beckons her to the centre of the room. She takes off the robe – awaits his instruction. The next ten minutes are filled with two-minute poses. She stands, arms outstretched like a ballerina, then sits, one leg bent under her, other knee drawn to her chest. She stares into the distance, hears the rub of charcoals on paper – rustle of new sheets mounted on easels. Finally, Jim instructs her to lie on the mattress, one arm beneath her head, other hand resting on her pelvis. The warmth from the heater fans her skin – makes her think of nights naked by an open fire. 'I could draw you', he'd said as he ran his open palm along the contour of her body. And he had. A portrait that now lay discarded amongst a pile of canvases in the spare room.

She dresses hurriedly when the class has ended. When she re-emerges the studio is empty, the students gone. She pulls her backpack over her shoulders. The instructor thanks her, pays her fee and asks how she's getting home.

'Walking', she says. 'I live close by'.

'Right you are. I'll see you Thursday, Mary. Mind how you go'.

'Molly', she says.

'What?'

'My name is Molly'.

A cold blast of air hits her as she opens the door. She steps out into the white glare of the snow and pulls on her red beret. Then she sees him, standing at the other side of the road, waiting.

'I thought I'd missed you', he says.

She gives no explanation. She imagines him watching the students file out of the centre thinking that maybe she'd gone. Jake blows on his fingers, rubs them together before shoving them in the pockets of his coat.

'They say it's to worsen in the next few days'.

'It's pretty', she says. They walk on in silence until they reach the house.

She lingers on the doorstep when he goes inside, stands with her back to the warmth from the hall. She hears him clatter round the kitchen. A few minutes later he puts his head out the door.

'Are you coming in, Moll?' he asks.

'In a minute'.

He pulls the porch door closed behind her. She stands with her arms folded and looks at the sky. There'll be a fresh fall tonight, she thinks, and all his hard work will be undone.

She passes the closed living room door. Inside, voices on the television. She climbs the stairs, opens the door to the spare room and switches on the ceiling light. The paintings are in a corner facing the wall. She looks through them – finds the one she wants and sits there staring at it. She wonders if that is how she looked to the artists tonight – or if this image was merely Jake's vision of her. She remembers how she teased him about hanging it on the living room wall. He was scandalised, said he wouldn't have the world look upon her naked. That was his privilege only. Now he recoils from her – his beautiful, flawed wife.

Molly takes the canvas and brings it into their bedroom. She goes downstairs, takes a hammer and rummages in the drawer for a picture hook. She hangs the picture in the centre of the wall – perfectly viewed from their bed. Then she stands back to look at it. She *will* make him remember. He can't go on punishing her for something that is not her fault.

He comes to bed sometime after midnight. She's been lying sleepless. Several times she got up to peer beneath the blind to see if the snow had started. In the back yard the trampoline is covered with a coating of white. It hasn't been used since the previous summer when Jake's niece Isabelle came to stay. Three days of watching Princess Sophia on DVD, of Jake jumping like a mad man on the trampoline – his exuberance a match for any four-year-old. He'd attempted to draw the child, though she never sat still long enough. In the end he took a photo – Izzy sat on the back step in an orange pinafore and yellow Wellington boots. Despite it being summer, she couldn't be coaxed out of them. Summer now seems a very long time ago.

Molly wakes to the vision of her naked self. On Jake's side, the sheet is cold. She wonders if he saw her portrait when he woke, is relieved to at least find it still hanging. The fresh fall hasn't come. Yesterday's snow remains piled in soiled heaps on the front lawn. Molly goes into the kitchen and fills the kettle. She opens the back door and steps outside. The bird feeder is empty. She refills it, watched by a curious robin that hops onto the table as soon as she's done. The snow is unsullied in the garden, her footsteps to the feeder the only blemish on the perfect white mantle. She thinks of Izzy playing in the garden, blonde ringlets bouncing. 'Imagine how tiring it'll be when we have our own', Jake had said. She'd smiled and said nothing as he scooped Izzy up and swung her by the ankles, the child squealing in delight.

Molly crosses to the trampoline and scoops snow from its base. It makes a satisfyingly powdery scrunch as she compacts it between her palms. She gathers and packs snow until a white mound dominates the garden. Her hands are warm now, face flushed with exertion. Half an hour later the snowman has formed – complete with a blue plaid scarf of Jake's and a beanie. She stands back and admires her work. The snowman looks at her, unblinking. She knows what Jake is going through, but it's not easy for her either. He should know that.

She spends the afternoon cooking. At times she is surprised when she catches sight of the snowman through the window. When it gets dark, she switches on the outside light so that the garden is illuminated. Jake comes home at six o'clock. She's lit candles and laid the table. A chicken casserole simmers in the oven and she's baked a chocolate cake. He ignores his place at the table, sits on the sofa and turns the television on. Molly dishes out the food.

'Jake', she says.

'I'll eat here if that's ok'.

He turns back to the news. Snowploughs are clearing a road somewhere in the midlands. She looks at the table, at the bottle of red wine, uncorked, next to the candle. She won't make a fuss. Instead she takes both their plates, puts them on the coffee table and pulls it nearer the sofa. She pours the wine and sits next to him, recalling how they used to love nights like this – huddled by the fire, impervious to the cold outside.

Jake compliments her on the food. She pours more wine and moves closer to him on the sofa. He is more talkative tonight. She sees it as promising. He even asks her what the life drawing class was like.

'Ah, you know', she says. 'It'll take time to get the hang of it. I won't be anywhere near as good as you anyway'.

She steals a sly look at him, but he doesn't comment on the addition to their bedroom wall.

'Who's teaching the class?' he asks.

'Some guy called Jim'.

She tightens her grip on the wine glass, suddenly afraid that Jake might know him – the art world is a small enough circle, but he makes no comment.

That night Jake is tired. He says he'll put the bins out before going to bed. Lately, he's been staying downstairs until she's asleep. She puts their dishes in the sink and then goes upstairs. She hears him out the back, the rattle of the bins as he wheels them round the side of the house and his boots in the snow. Quickly, she lights candles – scatters them round the room and turns the lamp out. She undresses down to her underwear – sits on the edge of the bed and waits.

She hears the back door being shut – the sound of him turning the key in the lock. He'll be checking that everything is switched off, that the guard has been placed safely in front of the fire. Her heart quickens when she hears his foot on the stairs. He appears in the doorway, takes in the candles but says nothing. Molly stands up, crosses the room and stands before him. She puts her hands on his chest and kisses him. She kisses his face, her hands find the buckle of his belt. He stills her fingers with his.

'I can't', he says.

He avoids her eyes – pivots roughly away from her.

She puts a hand on his arm. 'You can't keep doing this', she says. 'Can't you even look at me anymore? Jake!'

He exits the room without a word. She hears the door of the spare room close behind him. She blows the candles out and turns the lamp on. She takes her dressing gown from the hook on the back of the door, goes into the landing and considers following him into the room to have it out with him – but how many times have they been over it before? There is nothing she can say this time to make it any different.

No light shines from beneath the door of the spare room. Jake has got into bed in darkness. She returns to their room, slips off her dressing gown and gets beneath the covers. Her portrait taunts her and so she turns out the light and lies sleepless in the gloom.

In the morning he is gone before she wakes. She goes downstairs to make coffee. There has been a fresh fall of snow overnight – Jake's car is still in the driveway. He must have taken the train. She is by the sink rinsing the cafetière when she notices the absence of the snowman. His remains, hard lumpy snow and a spot of orange in the glare of white, the carrot she'd given him for a nose. She recalls having heard Jake moving about during the night and wonders, sadly, if there is any getting past this. That afternoon she goes outside and rebuilds the snowman, adorns it with her red beret and fixes her red gloves to his stick arms.

She and Jake avoid each other all of that day and the next. He doesn't arrive home until after she has gone to bed and she wonders where he has been. He sleeps in the spare room and is gone before she wakes. On the second day the snowman is still standing, but she doesn't get any satisfaction from this small triumph. The only thing that will make her happy is their life back and he will not grant her that.

In the evening she leaves the house before Jake returns. The snow is more than ankle deep. It wets the ends of her jeans through. She's trudged halfway to the art centre before she realises that she's forgotten her rucksack, but she doesn't want to turn back. Besides, the robe is not a necessity – she can enter the studio without.

'If you could just turn a little to the right, Molly. And move your other hand like this'.

Jim touches her fingers lightly, moves her into position. She stares at a potted plant in the corner of the room, tries to recite a poem in her head, but she has difficulty getting beyond the first verse. She thinks of that day in the surgery when she'd been afraid to meet Jake's gaze, eyes fixed instead on a chart on the wall – a map of the female anatomy.

'Have you ever had any procedures, Molly?' the doctor had asked. She'd hesitated, palm moving rhythmically over her abdomen, trying to ease the pain which had worsened since Jake had bundled her into the car. She'd kept her eyes focused on the chart.

'I had a termination, but it was almost twenty years ago'.

The sound of the doctor's pen scratching across the page as the pain shot through her stomach. 'And were there any complications?'

'No, I don't think so. I don't remember, I was young'. 'Fifteen' she wanted to add, but she knew it wouldn't make a difference – to the doctor or to Jake.

She was sent to the hospital that afternoon for a pelvic ultrasound which confirmed the doctor's suspicions – ectopic pregnancy.

'She's pregnant?' Jake had said, a guttering of hope, as soon extinguished by a shake of the doctor's head.

'The fertilized egg is in the fallopian tube. It must be terminated'.

'We're done, Molly'. She looks up, startled. The students have begun to pack their materials away. Jim looks at her, questioningly. She dresses in the back room. When she emerges Jim is still there talking to one of the women from the class. She smiles and says goodnight. When she steps out into the glare of the snow, the street is empty. Jake has not come to walk her home tonight. She walks slowly. Snowflakes drift and catch in her hair. It has been snowing off and on all afternoon. As she approaches the house, she sees that Jake has returned. The lights are on and beneath the sitting room blind she can see the television flashing. She opens the door and steps into the warmth of the hall. She unwinds her scarf, takes her coat off and hangs both on the end of the banister. He looks up when she enters the room, picks up the remote control and mutes the television.

How was the class?' he says.

'It was ok. I couldn't really concentrate'. She stands by the door, searches his face. There's something hard in his stare.

Jake leans over the edge of the sofa and produces her rucksack. The zip is open, her robe visible through the gap. She notices then, her sketchpad lying on the coffee table.

'Why, Molly?'

He stands up and thrusts the rucksack into her hands. He picks up the sketchpad, flicks through its empty pages and slams it down on the table again.

'Did you think I wouldn't find out? Jesus, Molly. You must think I'm some kind of fool'.

She shrugs, blood rushing to her face. She should have returned for the stupid bag. Should have known he'd be curious enough to look.

'I didn't think it was a big deal', she says.

'A big deal? You didn't think ... but that's the problem, isn't it? You don't think. You don't think, Molly. All you think about is yourself'.

She shakes her head. 'That's not fair. And you know it'.

He paces the room, stops before the fireplace. In silence, he stares into the embers.

'You're an artist, Jake. You know there's nothing in it. It's a life drawing class, for God's sake. Did you ever hear me complaining when you took a class – when you sat and stared at naked women? You're being ridiculous – and you know it'.

'But why? Why did you have to do it when you know how much it bothers me?'

He moves from the fire, stands with his back to the window – and looks at her properly for the first time in several months.

Molly takes off her coat, sits on the edge of the sofa. She is silent for a moment staring into the flames.

'Lately, I haven't been feeling good, since that day at the hospital, when I think of the way you looked at me, the way you haven't been able to touch me since. Have you any idea how ugly that makes me feel? Maybe this sounds stupid, but I needed someone to look at me – to make me feel – whole. Not like some faulty product cast aside – because that's how I've been feeling, Jake – ugly. I never thought you'd make me feel like that'.

'I didn't mean to'. He kicks at the carpet, arms crossed.

'You can't keep punishing me, Jake'.

'I'm not. I'm just afraid, Molly. Afraid. What if it happens again? You heard what the doctor said ... a twenty per cent chance'.

'And there's an eighty per cent chance that it won't. Now I'm willing to take that risk if you will. The question is do you love me enough to try?'

'You know I do'.

'Then stop pushing me away'. She reaches out a hand. He takes it, raises it to his lips and kisses her fingers. She puts her arms around his neck and he relents, his head on her shoulder.

'I should've told you about the abortion. It was wrong. But the doctor says it might not be to blame, that it can happen to anyone'.

She kisses his face, finds his lips and kisses them, too. He strokes her hair and pulls her to him. Eyes closed, she listens to the chaotic beating of his heart. She doesn't ask the question she fears the most – it is enough for now that he is here. And that they are willing to try.

The Fever

The man holds the boy's prayer book way above his head. The pages flap as he waves it back and forth, the spine in danger of snapping. The boy watches, silent. He hopes that the photo doesn't fall from between the pages. He wishes his father would stop, but he is too scared to say anything, too scared to move.

'Have you not had enough of this nonsense?' his father yells.

He is always yelling now. The boy stands in the corner, he feels his legs buckle and summons all his strength to stand.

'What has your God ever done for this family?' his father says.

His boots leave a trail of dried mud on the carpet as he paces the floor. It crumbles under his feet as he retraces his steps, stamping it into the ground. The child averts his eyes. He wishes his mother were here. He longs for her gentle voice. He glances at the empty frame where her photo used to be.

The man's voice has grown louder. He stops in front of the boy and roars. Spittle grazes his face and he turns his head to the side. 'Look at me when I'm talking to you …'

His father grabs him and jerks him by the arm. He yelps with pain as the large fist closes on his bony forearm.

'You're hurting me'.

'What did you say?'

The boy doesn't answer. His father yanks his arm again. Then suddenly he lets go.

The boy reels and grabs the back of the chair for balance. Quickly his father moves round to where he stands. He grabs him by the shoulder and pulls him towards the door.

'I don't want to hear another sound out of you, do you hear me?'

He swings the back door open and shoves the boy out into the rain.

'Stand there and don't move', he thunders.

The boy stands in the rain and prays. Water drips from his hair, runs down his face in rivulets. 'Our Father who art in heaven, hallowed be thy name'. He repeats the prayer silently, over and over, mouthing the words as the rain runs down the back of his school shirt and into his pants. Through a chink in the curtains he can see the light. He daren't move too close in case his father should see him. He's not sure which is worse – standing out here in the rain – or being in there with him, not knowing what will happen next.

The boy fingers a set of rosary beads in his pocket. He keeps them there always. His fingers close round each bead through the thick fabric of his school trousers as he mouths ten Hail Marys, his eyes closed against the rain. He wonders if his mother is looking down on him through the rain-drenched sky, grey clouds disguising her pretty face, her warm smile. He opens his eyes and blinks the rain away. A decade of the rosary said, he creeps towards the window. The room is empty.

Carefully, the boy lowers the handle of the door. It creaks and he stops, but all is quiet within. He enters the kitchen. There is not a sound except the ticking of the wall clock. His clothes drip on the tiled floor; already a puddle is forming where he stands. His prayer book lies on the kitchen table. He lifts the legs of his trousers clear of his shoes and quietly crosses the room. He opens the black leather cover and is relieved to find the photograph still there, the book undamaged bar some creasing to the spine. He takes the book and quietly walks towards the hall. In the doorway he pauses; he hears his father's heavy snores coming from the front room. Quickly, he passes the open door and hurries up the stairs. In his room he exhales a long breath, kicks off his shoes and pulls his sodden pullover over his head. He hangs it over the radiator to dry. He peels off his socks, throws them in the wash basket that hasn't been emptied since his mother died. A stale smell of laundry assaults him as he lifts the lid. He throws the offending garments in and replaces it quickly. Then he flings himself on the bed, naked.

He opens the book again, takes the photograph from between the pages. It is a picture of him and his mother, both smiling toward the camera past the lens at the photographer – his father – some years ago. He doesn't remember that day, but he remembers how happy they were on occasions like this. His father used to take them on trips up the mountains. He would come into his room early in the morning and wake him, 'come on boy-o', he'd say, 'rise and shine'. Downstairs his mother would be preparing a picnic, cutting sandwiches and filling a flask with tea. She always put the milk in a separate container to prevent the tea getting cold. Then there would be cakes for afterwards, topped with pink icing. These she would wrap carefully and place on top in the basket to prevent them from being crushed.

The boy begins to shiver and crawls beneath the blankets. His wet hair soaks the pillow and he pulls the blankets tighter round him. Rain beats against the windowpane, relentless. He cannot get warm. He burrows deeper, rubs his feet together and curls tightly beneath the covers foetus-style. His father used to read him stories when he went to bed. Now he falls asleep to dream strange hallucinatory dreams.

He wakes feverish. His forehead is damp; his hair clings to his sweaty brow. There is a dull throbbing like a jackhammer in his head. He tries to move but his limbs are reluctant. He lies there, half awake, half asleep. Light pours through a gap in the curtains. He hears his father rise, the sound of his feet on the hard boards as he bumps about in the next room. A door opens and he hears him enter the bathroom to wash and shave. The boy wants to call out, he mumbles 'Daddy' too low for the man to hear, then falls into a restless slumber.

It is afternoon when he wakes again. He squints at the light, blinks as his eyes adjust. His father sits near the bed. He leans closer when the boy wakes.

'Here, drink this'.

It is difficult to sit up. He leans on his elbows and falls back against the pillow. His father helps him upright and puts the pillow behind his back. The cool air on his hot skin makes him tremble. He tries to control the unsteady chatter of his teeth. He takes the mug that his father offers; the liquid is hot and sweet – boiled lemonade. His father watches him drink it.

'How do you feel?' The man's voice is anxious, abrupt.

'I'm tired Daddy, and my head hurts'.

He leans over, puts a cool palm on the boy's forehead.

'You're burning up'.

The boy holds out the mug and his father takes it from him. He sinks beneath the covers, tiredness overcoming him. He finds it difficult to keep his eyes open, his father's image blurs and fades. He calls out for his mother. She doesn't come right away. He stops calling as consciousness fades.

In the dream he knows that he is dreaming. His mother is there and the priest. He sees himself too, but with a different face. It is like watching a film unfold. His mother is wearing a yellow dress. She smiles down at him and catches his hand. They are in the church and sunshine streams through the stained glass windows.

'I can't help out at the mass on Sunday', the boy tells the priest.

'That's a pity, Stephen. You're the best altar boy I've got. You'll make a fine priest one day'.

His mother squeezes his hand.

'I'm not sure I'm going to be a priest, father'.

'Oh'. The priest looks disappointed.

The boy hesitates. 'Daddy says God took Mammy away. That when I pray I'm not praying to anybody. That it's all nonsense'.

'Don't be saying things like that to the priest', his mother says. 'Nobody is taking anyone anywhere. I'm sorry father', she says. She scolds the boy and takes him by the hand out into the daylight. He can't feel his mother's hand anymore and he begins to get frightened. He tries to pull his hand away but a weightless grip seems to hold him. When he looks up it is a strange woman that holds his hand.

'Where's my Mammy?' the boy says.

He wakes sweating. He hears voices and struggles to open his eyes. The doctor sits on the edge of the bed. At first the boy thinks it's the priest.

'Can you sit up for me, Stephen?'

He moves into an upright position slowly, groggily. The doctor's stethoscope is cold against his skin.

'Can you take a deep breath for me?'

The boy takes a shuddering breath.

'And again?' the doctor says.

He looks in his mouth, tells him to say 'ah'. He takes his temperature. The boy doesn't like the feel of the thermometer beneath his tongue. He almost gags. Then the doctor tells him that he can cover himself up again. His head hurts as he lowers himself beneath the covers.

'He's caught a bad chill', the doctor says.

His father nods.

All night his father stays by him. When he wakes in darkness he hears his father's shallow breathing nearby. He has brought the blankets from his own bed and made up a bed on the floor. The boy lies awake for a long time in the dark. He thinks about his mother. He wonders what she was doing in the teacher's car. He tries to figure out why his father is so angry with God. When his Granny died his mother told him that she was gone to heaven. Didn't everyone go to heaven? Maybe his father was angry because she didn't take him with her; that she took the teacher instead. In the darkness Stephen reaches out a hand. He tips the bedside lamp and it rocks back and forth. He hears his father stir as his hand falls on the prayer book on the bedside locker. He eases it toward him beneath the covers, feels the space between the pages where he keeps the photograph. He thumbs it in darkness, imagining his mother's smiling face and falls asleep with the book held tightly to his chest. He thinks he feels his father standing over him in the night, feels the light touch of a hand brushing his hair from his forehead. He thinks he hears a voice say, 'I'm sorry, son', and he clutches the book tighter, unsure whether he is dreaming or whether the fever has broken at last.

Where Did You Go?

Joanna pulls into the car park. She puts the car into neutral, lifts the handbrake and sits there with the engine running. There is nobody around. She locks the doors, opens the glove compartment and takes out a packet of cigarettes. The box is tattered at the edges, a packet of Silk Cut Blue. She places one between her lips. It is more for something to do than for the cigarette itself. Her lighter flares in darkness.

She opens the window just enough to let the smoke out. The air feels damp, tinged with the faint smell of chlorine from the swimming pool. This, she thinks, is just outside the changing rooms. Above it the windows of the canteen mirror the blackened sky, the orange glow of the streetlamp. Oliver's car is parked by the security hut, an old BMW. He will be doing the rounds inside, his footsteps echoing in empty corridors, past the gym, the arts office. Perhaps he will stop in the corridor and look through the plate glass into the empty pool covered with blue tarpaulin.

It's after twelve. She will wait a little longer. She pushes her seat back and turns the radio on. Two women battle it out on a late night talk show. The host tries desperately to get a word in between the two. She switches it off and the engine purrs in silence. She drags on the cigarette butt, her fingers dangerously close to the tip. It glows crimson. She stubs it in the ashtray, pauses as she hears a sound in the distance. She listens to night sounds amplified in the frosty air. There it is again. A cough perhaps? Then silence. She flicks the cigarette butt out the window. She hates the smell of smoke in the car. Taking a quick look in the mirror she wipes her mouth with the back of her hand and pats her hair. Then she switches the engine off, takes the keys from the ignition and sprays her wrists with perfume before zipping up her bag.

Joanna steps out of the car and slams the door behind her. She hums a tune and can't place where she's heard it. The wind catches her full force as she turns the corner of the building, whips her hair from her face. She pulls her coat tighter and tucks her scarf beneath the collar. The grounds are floodlit. Trees nuzzle darkly round the edges of the football pitch, deserted. She quickens her step.

The lights are out in the main foyer. She tries the door. It's locked. She cups her hands against her refection and puts her face up close to the glass. She can see nothing inside but a red neon display flashing on a vending machine. Her breath fogs the glass. Behind her, footsteps sound on the pavement. She turns, raises a hand to shade her eyes from the glare of a flash lamp.

'Hey there'.

'Oliver. You frightened the life out of me', she says.

'Sorry. I thought I heard a car. I went around the other side ...' He waves his hand in the direction of the car park. The beam from the lamp dances across the pavement. She stands there, hands dug deep in her pockets.

'Do you want to come inside?' he says.

'Sure'.

Oliver takes a bunch of keys from his pocket, searches for the right one. She follows him into the building.

'We'll go up to the canteen', he says. 'I'll make us a mug of tea, warm us up'.

He leaves the lights off, shines the torch down the corridor. She follows close behind. There is nothing but the sound of their steps, their clothes rustling as they move. It reminds her of the college, nights when she has worked late. Something sinister about the emptiness, the cold brick walls. She shivers and grips the rail as Oliver takes the stairs two at a time in front of her.

'Be careful', he says.

She smiles in the dark. He hands her the torch and opens the door to the canteen. He presses a switch on the wall and the fluorescent light flickers above them. She closes her eyes.

'So what has you out so late?' he says.

'I was passing. I saw your car'.

'I take it your mother doesn't know you're here?'

'No'. She sits by the window, looks out over the car park. Oliver spoons coffee into a percolator.

'I'll have to use this', he says. 'The boiler's long switched off'.

She says nothing. He fills the jug with water and puts it back on the plate. He reaches into his pocket and takes out a packet of cigarettes.

'I thought you weren't supposed to smoke in here', she says.

'You're not'. He smiles. She watches his hands as he lights up, the way that his fingers grip the cigarette. His hands are soft like a woman's. His fingers are long and slender. Her mother has felt these hands.

'You want one?'

'Sure'. She wets her lips. He throws the packet on the table.

'Thanks', she says.

She swings back in the chair and puts one foot up on the table. She taps a cigarette from the box and lets it dangle from her mouth, unlit. 'Surprised to see me?' she asks.

'Sort of'. He looks at the floor. 'You know it's always nice to see you'.

'Nice? You can do better than that ...'

He laughs. She leans back further in the chair, lets her arms swing by her sides. She loosens the scarf from her throat, unbuttons her coat until it swings open. When she looks up, he is watching her.

'You never gave me a light', she says.

He takes the lighter from his pocket and pushes it across the table. She ignores it, rises and walks round to where he stands. She leans towards him and lights her cigarette from his.

'I didn't hear you come in'.

Joanna's mother glances up. She lays the table – two places. Joanna stands in the doorway.

'I finished early', she says. 'There wasn't much to do'.

'Well, you worked late enough yesterday anyway'.

Her mother continues to set the cutlery, head lowered. Joanna searches for any sign of recognition. She sees none.

'I went out', she says. 'Afterwards'.

On the cooker a pot spills over. The water hisses on the ring. She lifts the lid and looks into the pot. Steam burns her wrist. She curses under her breath, puts the lid back and holds her arm beneath the cold tap.

'So where did you go?'

'What?'

'Last night – where did you go?' her mother asks.

'Oh we ... we went out for a drink. You know, end of term and everything'.

She dries her arm with the towel. Her mother takes the lid off the pot and stabs the potatoes with a knife. She slides the pot from the cooker. Joanna spears a piece of chicken from her plate.

'Any plans for tonight?' she asks, casually.

'Oliver's taking me out', her mother says.

She heaps the plates with turnip. Joanna averts her eyes. She wanders across the room and picks up a magazine from the coffee table.

'Anywhere nice?' she says, turning the pages slowly.

'I don't know', her mother says. 'He says it's a surprise. He's full of surprises'.

Joanna smiles.

She's in her room when Oliver calls. She hears the drone of the engine, a snippet of music before the car door slams. She sits on the edge of her bed, counts his steps from the car until the doorbell rings. She eases her own door open and steps into the landing. Her mother takes a last look in the hall mirror and smoothes her clothes before she answers the door.

'Oliver, come in'.

'I won't', he says. 'I've left the car running'.

She can just see the tips of his shoes in the doorway, his shiny black lace-ups. She thinks she can smell his cologne. Her mother turns and takes her coat from the knob of the banister. Joanna steps back out of the light.

'I'm going, Joanna', her mother calls from the bottom of the stairs.

She doesn't answer. She stands still until she hears the door click shut. She hurries down the stairs and grabs her keys from the rack on the wall. Through the lace curtain she watches as Oliver opens the passenger door and her mother disappears from sight. When they've pulled away from the curb she opens the hall door. A bitter wind stirs the leaves in the driveway. They rustle beneath her feet. She walks as far as the gate. The taillights are red points now like the last embers of a burning coal. She stands there and watches as they grow fainter and fainter in the distance and finally vanish. Across the street a neighbour's television flashes through open curtains. A man stands in front of the fire, his hands behind him. She can see the back of his wife's head. She sits on the sofa beneath the window. The man is laughing, but where is the child? She cannot see. She turns away, folds her arms against the wind. She has never felt so lonely.

It is late when she hears the key turn in the lock. Her legs are cramped when she moves. Her circulation is slow. She listens for the sounds of voices, but hears none. Her mother is alone. She rubs her eyes with the back of her hand. She hadn't meant to sleep. She squints at the clock on the mantle – 2.35 am.

'You're late'.

Her mother doesn't answer. Joanna rises and feels her way towards the light switch. She bumps against the table and curses as light floods the room. She shades her eyes.

'Have a good time?' she asks.

She stretches, pulls one foot up behind her as she holds the arm of the chair. Her mother is quiet. She stands in the doorway, her back to the room.

'What did you do then? Go back to his place?'

'We talked'.

Joanna watches as her mother moves slowly out of the room. She is at the foot of the stairs, thinking whether to climb or stay.

'How could you?'

Joanna laughs. 'He told you then? He's even worse than I thought', she says. She rubs her hands on her trousers, leans against the jamb of the door. 'Did he tell you how many times we did it?'

Her mother turns, walks back down the two steps she's taken. She turns the light on. Her face is puffy like she's been crying. For the first time she looks old.

'He refused you, Joanna', she says.

Joanna turns away. 'Is that what he told you?' she says.

'It's what happened'.

Joanna says nothing. She wanders across the room. Her mother watches her retreat.

'Do you hate me that much?' she says.

'You mean you didn't notice'.

Joanna stands by the window. The lights have gone out in the house across the street, the family tucked safe in bed. She wonders again where the child is.

'You never noticed anything strange', she says. 'You never did'.

She lifts the lace curtain and stares into the night. A frost has formed on the grass. It sparkles on the roof of her car. Would she too have stiffened if she'd stayed outside?

'He lifted my nightdress and he rubbed himself up against me while you slept in your bed'.

'Oliver?' Her mother's voice is barely a whisper.

'No'.

In the glass with the lights behind her, her reflection stares and she cannot escape *his* eyes.

Her mother sobs on the stairs.

The Pilgrimage

I watched her struggle up the rocky mountainside, boots slipping on the stony surface as the wind whipped her hair into her face. She stopped and her whole body seemed to sway in the wind as she stood grabbing at the strands of hair that had come loose from beneath the collar of her bright blue windbreaker.

'Take my hand, Clara'.

From a grassy mound above her I reached out, the wind kept blowing the hood of my red anorak in front of me and I had trouble keeping my own balance though, as a keen climber in my college days, I was more used to these conditions than she was. We'd gone on some hikes together in the Dublin Mountains in the early days of our relationship. I figured that maybe that was the reason she'd suggested this weekend, to bring back whatever it was that had seemed to elude us in the past few months.

We'd arrived in Westport the night before. It was cold and windy and we had booked into the first B&B we'd come across just outside the town. We could've found a nicer place, I thought, but we'd argued on the way there and the atmosphere between us was taut. I didn't wish to strain it even further, which could easily, I knew, result in Clara slamming out of the car and traipsing with her bag over her shoulder along a darkened country road as I crawled alongside trying to coax and pacify her back into the car. It wouldn't be the first time.

I was right about the B&B. There were two single beds in a dull room that reminded me of the guestroom in my grandmother's house all those years ago. The walls were papered in a floral design. Both curtains and carpet were dark brown and the furniture heavy and antique. Clara sat on one of the single beds, pulled off her boots and announced that she was going to take a shower, she felt musty after the long journey in the car. I remembered a time when we'd showered together.

For some reason I thought about the first time we'd slept together. It was in a B&B on the harbour in the coastal town of Skerries just a mile from where I'd lived. She'd booked herself in to be near me when I was in the middle of separating from my wife. We'd spent stolen hours together when I was supposed to be working. In the evening before I'd dressed to return home we'd watched the lights come on in the harbour, shining in the water and making the dark shapes of the old boats look almost ghostly against the darkening sky.

The water continued to run. I got up and walked to the door. I could hear her singing softly to herself beneath the rush of the water. I pictured her body, pale and light. She had retained the weightlessness of youth. I moved away from the door, sat on the end of the bed and turned on the television. A few minutes later I turned it off again. It was quiet now in the bathroom. I stood looking at the two single beds and decided to push them together. The bathroom door opened just as I was fixing the duvets between the beds and Clara appeared dressed in her pyjamas with her hair still wet. I looked at her almost guiltily.

Clara threw back the covers and climbed into the bed nearest the door.

'So what time should we set off in the morning?' she said. She picked up her phone to set the alarm clock.

'As early as possible, I guess'. I undressed, threw my clothes over the armchair under the window and climbed into bed. I moved over towards Clara. She had her back to me, her hair was damp on the pillow and I found myself lying in the place where the two beds separated. I put my hand on her stomach and felt her muscles tighten.

'What's wrong?' I said.

'Nothing. I'm just tired, that's all'.

I began to caress her, my hand moving slowly over her smooth abdomen, but she didn't react and finally, without protest, I withdrew to my own bed and slept.

At breakfast the woman in the B&B advised us against climbing the Reek. She said that the forecast wasn't good and we ought to wait, but Clara scorned the woman's advice saying that we knew what we were doing. We'd be fine.

We set out early, parked in the car park at the foot of the mountain. There were few other climbers around. I had a sudden, foreboding sense that we shouldn't have come. As I stepped out of the car I scanned the rocky mountain before us. A few coloured dots moved in the distance. I looked at Clara. I couldn't remember the last time she'd climbed, nor could I understand her unwavering compulsion to do this.

About an hour into the climb she began struggling for breath, but her face was set in that way I'd seen so many times before when she was determined to do something.

'You ok?' I said.

'Fine'. She took my hand without glancing at my face, but as soon as she was on a level with me she pulled it away again.

'Hey, we don't have to go any farther if you don't want to, you know'. I raised my voice above the wind.

'I'm ok', she said. 'Let's just keep going'. She stormed ahead, feet slipping on the uneven surface, but she seemed compelled by some vigorous, internal resolve to reach the summit. I stayed close, knowing she was too proud to ask for anyone's help, even mine.

We climbed steadily for another half hour and when I gauged that we were about halfway to the summit I suggested we take a break. Clara seemed to have tapped into some hidden reservoir of energy since her initial difficulties, but at my suggestion she sat down on a heavy boulder and took a long drink from the flask. For a while we sat in silence staring down on the blues and greens of Clew Bay spread out beneath us. We could have been the only two people on the planet as we sat on that bleak mountainside and yet as I looked at Clara sitting on her rock a few feet away I felt between us an unfathomable divide.

'What was it that made you want to do this?'

Clara looked off into the distance and shrugged. 'I'd read about it. How people climbed this hill to atone for their sins'.

'And what sins have you committed, Clara?' I laughed as I said it, but Clara didn't respond. She stood up and paced a few steps amongst the rocks as she stared down at the bay far, far below.

'I wanted things to get back to normal with us, you know? But I don't think we ever can. It's me. I've ruined everything. I don't know what it is, I destroy everything that's good'.

I felt my heart beat faster as her voice rose and drifted on the wind. I wondered if her words were heard on the bay below, if they were carried to distant places where people spoke in foreign tongues.

'Come on. Everyone goes through rough patches, Clara. It's normal. We've just got to stick together'.

'You don't understand', she said.

She was right. I didn't. I didn't know what had happened to change everything between us, but I knew, just as she did, that things hadn't been the same. As I listened to her words I knew that it wasn't the weather that had caused my earlier sense of foreboding. It was this moment that I'd known was coming, but which I'd been strenuously trying to avoid.

'Then tell me', I said. 'Tell me what's changed'.

Clara sat down again, but this time she sat opposite me. She looked at the rocks at her feet and she began to speak. 'There was someone else. It was a few months ago and it only happened once, but I can't get it out of my head. I'm sorry'.

'What? How could you? I mean – you – you went crazy every time I mentioned a female friend ... Clara!' I stood and began to pace up and down the mountainside unable to take it in.

'I'm sorry', she said again.

I stopped in front of her. 'What?'

'I said I'm sorry. I don't know what else to say. Why don't we just continue on. It's getting late'.

'You want to continue? You just tell me this out of the blue and expect me to accept it ... what's wrong with you?' Suddenly I needed to know the details. 'When did this happen? Where?' I asked.

'You remember that party, the one you wouldn't go to. I was meeting some friends from college'.

'So you're blaming me now? Just because I didn't want to go to one of your stupid parties, you're trying to say it's my fault. Jesus, I thought I could trust you, Clara'.

'You never want to go anywhere', she said. 'Not with me'.

'That's not true. You know I've nothing to say to these people. You never had a problem with it before'.

Clara stood up. I could see that her expression had changed. She looked defensive, angry even. 'Oh, don't pretend that you're so innocent', she said. 'What about that French teacher in your last job? We all know you had a thing for her, don't we? Only she didn't want anything to do with you, Greg'.

Clara was already moving away from me. I followed her and put a hand on her arm. For a moment I thought she looked frightened. Maybe she figured I'd gone crazy. There was no one around, no one there to witness what I might do to her, but I felt this terrible emptiness inside and revulsion that she could be scared of me.

'The only thing that happened with Claudette was in your sordid little imagination'.

The lie hung between us as we stood on that windy mountainside. My hand was still on her arm and neither of us had moved.

'Who was he?' I asked.

'Just a guy I knew at college'.

I let go of her arm. We stood like that for some time, neither of us knowing what to do next. I was surprised when Clara raised a hand to wipe some tears away.

'You know what the worst thing is', she said. 'If he'd wanted me, I wouldn't be here now. But he didn't. And I tried to forget. I tried to be with you, like we used to be, but nothing seems to work'.

A group of walkers was coming down the hill, making their way back from the summit. One of the men indicated with a pole towards the top. 'I wouldn't go any further', he said, 'it's starting to blow a real gale up there'. I thanked him for the advice. Clara stood, her back to us both and didn't turn. I thought of that night with Claudette and I tried to reconcile it in my head with Clara's betrayal, but I couldn't. Her guilt was something loathsome, it made her weak. She was looking out across the bay now, face streaked where the tears had caused her make-up to run. Suddenly she began to move again, head bowed, into the squall. 'Clara, don't', I said, but either she didn't hear or didn't heed my words. I stood for a long time tracking Clara's blue windbreaker up the side of that mountain – the gulf between us too wide now ever to be closed.

SAYING GOODBYE TO BETTINA

'Where've you been?'

Scott's mother stood in the doorway drying her hands with the striped tea towel.

'Nowhere', he said.

'You've been nowhere for a long time', she said. 'What have you been doing?'

Scott flopped down on the sofa and picked up the TV remote control. His mother stood there for a moment and when it became clear that he wasn't going to answer she flung the tea towel over her shoulder and left the room.

'Dinner will be ready at seven', she called. 'And get those runners down off the sofa'.

Scott sighed and put his feet down. He slunk down in the cushions, not really looking at the figures that bounced around the basketball court on the screen in front of him. Instead he was thinking about Bettina and the way she had pretended not to see him at school. He hadn't made a big deal about it. Instead, he had tried to smile at her to show that everything was ok, that he didn't care, but she had walked straight past him in the corridor, head held high, as though his existence was something of which she was completely unaware. At that moment he felt as though she'd driven a knife through his gut.

After dinner Scott went up to his room. He lay on the bed staring at the cluster of luminous stars stuck to his ceiling and wondered why she'd done it – sent him that stupid text message to tell him that it wasn't really 'working out', that she needed more time for her studies. She could've told him to his face, he reasoned. They could have talked about it and worked something out. It was true that until a week ago, when she'd seemingly begun to avoid him, they had spent almost every day together for the past five months, but his studies had not suffered and he didn't think that hers had either. In fact he had been helping her with maths, which she wasn't so good at and her grades had visibly improved.

There was a knock on the bedroom door. Before Scott could say anything the door opened and light from the landing came flooding into the darkened room. He reached out a hand to turn on the light on his bedside locker as Pete, his little brother, trundled across the room waving a Playstation game over his head telling him that he had to try it, that it was the best game ever.

Scott sat up on the bed as Pete raised one short leg and scrambled up on top of the covers. The mattress wobbled as he bounced around holding the game out to Scott while telling him about the dragons and how you had to slay them to save the princess.

'What if I don't want to save her?' Scott said.

Pete looked confused.

'But she's captured by the dragon and there are all these other monsters and they've got swords and magic and …'

'Ok, ok', said Scott. 'Let's play it'.

Pete won every game. It wasn't because Scott allowed him to. It was because his mind kept wandering to Bettina. He'd followed her home after school that day, not so that she would see him, but at a distance. He'd even taken a shortcut through the park in order to arrive at the house before her, but somewhere between the park gates through which he'd entered, and those on the other side through which he'd emerged, he'd lost Bettina. He'd positioned himself behind a wall at the corner of the block of houses where she lived, satisfied that he would catch sight of her at any moment, but after an hour standing there she hadn't arrived and finally he'd given up hope.

'Bam! Take that sucker', Pete veered with the console as he blasted the dragon with some sort of fire gun. He bounced up and down with glee as the dragon fell to his knees and the princess came running from the cave. Just then Scott's phone rang. He pounced on it, almost knocking Pete from his perch on the bed, but when he looked at the screen Bettina's name did not show up, instead it was Derek, a friend of his from school. He didn't feel like talking to anyone, so he pressed the 'reject' button and threw the phone on the bed.

'Ok, buddy. I'm all gamed out', he told Pete. 'I've got homework to do and so do you'.

Pete moaned and climbed down from the bed. He took his game from the computer and half ran out of the room, making machine gun noises as he went.

Scott sat down at his desk and took out his maths book. He tried to concentrate on equations. He took out his copybook and began to work out the first sum, but he kept looking at the mobile phone on his desk wishing it would ring. Finally he threw down his pen and picked up the phone. He stood up, walked to the window and back again. Before he had time to think about it too much he dialled her number. He paced the room as the phone rang.

It rang and rang until finally he heard her soft, buttery voice. 'Hi, this is Bettina. Leave a message!' There was a bleep, but Scott didn't say anything. Instead he threw the phone against the wall.

'Scott, what are you doing up there?'

Scott didn't answer his mother's question. He pictured her standing in the hallway staring up through the banisters. Then he heard her call him again.

'Scott?'

He opened the door. 'It's ok. I just dropped my encyclopaedia', he said.

He went back into the room and closed the door. He went over to the window and looked out through the telescope that his mother had given him last year for his fifteenth birthday. With his eye close to the lens he could make out some constellations. He saw Sirius, the Dog Star, twinkling brightly, and beside it, its diminished comrade the White Dwarf. He stared out into this vast space of the universe and as he did so he wondered what it would be like just to vanish off the earth.

That night he slept badly. He kept dreaming about his father. He would wake up and fall asleep again only to continue the same dream. Eventually he sat up and turned on the light. He tried to read his Tolkien book to stay awake but his mind kept wandering and he couldn't concentrate on the story. What had happened with Bettina, or more to the point what had *not* happened with Bettina, had brought back all the old memories about his father leaving. He'd been ten years old at the time and Pete had not even been born. Pete had never met their father. He was, in fact, their father's unwitting going away present to their mother. Before he'd even known that his wife was pregnant with their second child, he had gone.

Scott's mother had cried for what seemed like a year. He would come in from school to find her chopping vegetables at the kitchen sink and even before she'd turned to him he knew that the tears were spilling down her cheeks, falling on her hands and on the chopping knife that she held poised above the carrots. She'd ask him how school was, smiling through the tears and he'd drop his school bag, give her a quick hug and pretend that she wasn't always crying. When Pete was born she'd cried too, but this was a different type of crying and somehow it was Pete that put an end to his mother's tears. Sometimes he was jealous about that, but he told himself not to be stupid. Pete was a fat, happy baby that everybody loved and he guessed his mother didn't have time to think about the things that made her cry after Pete came along.

The next morning when Scott's mother tapped on the door and told him it was time to get up, Scott pulled the covers over his head and ignored her. He had already hit the 'snooze' button on his alarm clock three times.

'Scotty. Come on, you're late', his mother said. 'It's 8.15'.

This time she'd stuck her head around the door. Downstairs he could hear Pete making robot sounds while he ate his cornflakes. He pushed the cover down so that his mother could hear him speak.

'I'm not going to school today, Mam. I don't feel well'.

His mother came over to the bed and looked at him. She put her hand on his forehead. It was cool against his skin and he wished that she would leave it there.

'What's wrong, Scotty? Can I get you anything?'

He shook his head. 'No, I've just got a headache', he said.

This was partially true. He had a throbbing in his left temple that had started during the night and wouldn't leave him alone, but more than that he couldn't face school. He couldn't bear the thought of meeting Bettina in the corridor on his way to class and for her to ignore him again. His mother got him some Aspirin and a glass of water. He swallowed the tablets down dutifully and lay there with the curtains drawn.

When he awoke again he was surprised to find that it was afternoon. He got out of bed and pulled the curtains back. Light poured through the window, a late autumnal sun that painted everything in its golden light. Scott opened the door and stepped into the landing. He crept two steps down the stairs and peered through the banister.

'Mam?' he called, but the only sound he heard downstairs was the ticking of the clock in the hallway.

In his room he dressed in jeans and his favourite Red Hot Chilli Peppers t-shirt. He guessed that his mother had brought Pete to the tennis club where he went every Tuesday and Thursday afternoon. He slipped out of the house and walked in the direction of the school. Classes would be finishing soon and he wanted to be there to catch sight of Bettina.

At precisely 3.45 the bell rang and the students began to file out, a noisy mob, which Scott watched from a safe distance through the railings at the side of the building. He saw his classmates emerge, heard their usual shouts of camaraderie. Then he saw Bettina. She came out with the usual group of girls. He thought about approaching her. Perhaps she would allow him to walk her home and they could work things out, but even as he began to walk in the direction of the school gates, he saw Bettina wave goodbye to her friends and depart in the opposite direction with a boy that Scott knew to see, but had never spoken to.

The boy was tall and was older than the rest of them. Scott reckoned he must've been one of the sixth years. He put his arm around Bettina as they walked away and she laughed at something he'd said. Suddenly the world turned. Scott gripped the railing, his head light. Yellow spots clouded his vision. He closed his eyes until the feeling passed and when he opened them again Bettina and the boy were distant figures, her red school bag the distinguishing feature on which his eyes focused. For a moment he contemplated following them, but what would he say? He didn't want to end up looking like a complete idiot. No, he would think of a way to punish Bettina for what she'd done.

For the rest of the evening Scott stayed in the backyard. He bounced his basketball round and shot hoops, and all the time he deliberated his plan to punish Bettina. He stayed outside until it got dark. His mother put her head out the door and told him it was time he quit, that she had put Pete to bed and she didn't want him woken by the racket. He went inside and began to gather the things that he needed to put his plan into action.

It was after eleven when he climbed into the lowest branch of the Chapman's Chestnut tree. He'd sneaked out of the house whilst his mother was taking her nightly shower. He'd already said goodnight and surprised his mother by kissing her cheek, something he'd not done in a long time. Then he'd taken his rucksack, into which he'd thrown the things he needed and made his way down the street to where Bettina's family lived.

Now Scott sat in the tree in the Chapman's front garden and stared across at the house. There was a light on in the living room but the curtains were drawn and he could not see into the room where he imagined Bettina's parents sat watching TV. Just above him Bettina's room was in darkness. He imagined all the times he'd been in that room, listening to music or helping Bettina with her homework. He contemplated throwing a stone at the window but that was not why he was here. He was here to rid himself of the hurt that had entrenched itself within him from the moment that he realised it was over.

From his place in the tree, Scott watched the Chapman's cat stroll across the lawn. It stopped and stood there in the moonlight and for a moment he wondered if it sensed his presence above it, but then it moved on, intent on its night wanderings, unaware of his existence.

It was quiet in the tree. For the first time in the last couple of days Scott felt a strange peace descend upon him. He looked at Bettina's window again, imagined her sleeping face. Her dreams unspoilt by conscience. Quietly he unzipped his bag, took out the towrope that he'd taken from his mother's car and threw it like a lasso around the branch above him. He sat there, the rope dangling lightly next to him in the chilly air. Above him the cloudless sky revealed the stars that he looked at so often through his telescope. How far did the world stretch, he wondered. He continued to stare at the sky as his hands moved lightly on the rope. He cast one more glance at her darkened window and he wasn't sure if he imagined the curtain twitching, or if it was the movement of his body gradually sliding from the branch that made him think that it had moved.

Mr Pepper

'Hey, hey you there! Wake up. You can't sleep there!'

Maxim opened his eyes and blinked the face, looming above him, into focus. Bleached hair, cobalt eyes, lashes clumped by layers of black, lips redder than red and beyond her so much light. Where was he? He stretched and tried to move into a sitting position, muscles aching from too many hours spent on the hard tiled floor. Then he remembered the events of the previous night and how he'd ended up there. 'I'm sorry. Please – what time is it?'

The woman straightened, tugged at the cuff of her leather jacket to check a silver wristwatch. 'Seven am. What are you doing here? Have you no place to go?'

He looked beyond her, through the plate glass of the outer door. The rain that had driven him to seek shelter the previous night continued to beat the pavement, moiling clouds offering no respite. Maxim shivered and started to his feet. His bladder ached and his right arm, which the man had twisted behind him, protested as he bent to gather the solitary blanket and stuff it into his old blue sports bag. 'I'm sorry, I go now', he said. He hadn't intended to sleep so long, thought he'd have packed up and left before any of the residents of the apartment complex had discovered him. His clothes, damp still, clung to his skin and he felt the cold, bone-deep, as he drew the bag across his back.

'Where will you go?' the woman said.

He shrugged and waited for her to move from the doorway, but she continued to block his exit, cobalt eyes studying him almost hungrily. 'What's your name?' she asked.

'Virgil'. It was the name of his younger brother.

'Look – I'll tell you what, why don't you come upstairs? You can wait till the rain stops'.

He looked at her, doubtful – but it was unlikely that the story had hit the news – if it would at all. It was Sunday and the papers had gone to print the night before. He shivered again and nodding followed the woman inside the building.

On the stairs they met no one. They traipsed up to the third floor. On the landing, light shone through a porthole window that looked out across the promenade. The woman took a bunch of keys from her coat pocket and pushed open the door to her apartment. 'Come in', she told him when he hesitated on the threshold. A cloying smell, sweet and woody hung heavily in the air. On a small table he spotted the origin, a vase loaded with incense sticks – grey ash spilling onto the table's surface. A thump on the other side of a closed door startled him. He looked to the woman, about to ask if there were someone else there when a low growl sounded and then erupted in a cacophony of barking.

'He doesn't like strangers', the woman said. She opened a door and pointed into a chaotic room piled with boxes. 'You can sit in here'. She left, closing the door behind her. A moment later he heard the dog snuffing under it. 'Sit,

Mr Pepper', the woman said. 'Good dog'. Startled, the man looked round. With the dog outside, he was a prisoner. What if the news had broken after all? What if the result of last night's debacle had turned out direr than he'd thought and the woman was calling the police?

He crossed the room to a small window. It looked onto a cement wall and a narrow alleyway beneath – at best he'd break a leg from the drop. He put his ear to the door – immediately the dog began snuffing again. He heard the rattle of delft and then the woman telling the dog to stay back. He caught a glimpse of the huge black beast before the door shut.

'There – I figured you must be hungry'. The woman set down a tray with a mug of tea, some bread and cheese. 'I'm sorry about the dog outside the door, it's just ... how do I know you wouldn't try to rob or rape me? You can't be too careful, a woman on your own'.

The man took a piece of bread. 'I wouldn't hurt you', he said. He didn't tell her that what she said made little sense. If he'd intended to do her harm, he could do so now in minutes without the dog to protect her. She cleared a spot on the bed, sat and watched him while he ate. He figured she was mid-thirties, a strongly-built woman, not unattractive. Her eyes, the first thing he'd noticed, really were a hypnotic shade of blue. Her short hair, bleached white, was dark at the roots.

'Where are you from?' she asked.

'Moldova'.

'Your English is good'.

'Not so good, I learn in streets'. He ate hungrily, glad of the hot tea. The woman stood up, opened a chest of drawers and took out a man's hooded top and chinos. 'You can put these on', she said.

'Whose are they?' he asked.

'Nobody's. He's gone'. She watched him examine the clothes. She took the trousers and held them to his waist. 'You'll need a belt', she said. 'You're too thin'. He was thin. He'd lost weight in the past month – had been sleeping rough for as long. He'd spent a few nights in a hostel until he'd almost been pricked by a used needle caught in the blanket. After that he decided it was safer outdoors.

'Go on', she said. 'Put them on'. He hesitated. 'What? Haven't you ever undressed before a woman?'

He thought of Daria. It had been what, nine months since he'd seen her? A vision of her sat astride him, long dark hair swaying in his face, her body lithe as a girl's. God, how he still wanted her. He had taken off the dirty black t-shirt and was sitting with the sweater the woman had given him resting on his knees. The vision of his wife passed and he found the woman staring at him, amused. 'Come on, make yourself decent', she said. She tossed the chinos on the bed, stood and made her way to the door.

'The toilet', he said. 'I need ...'

She pointed to a bucket in the corner of the room. 'You can use that'. She turned to the window where the rain beat relentlessly against the glass. 'That's not going to let up. There's no point in you leaving to end up in someone else's porch. I've to go out, but I'll be back in a few hours. The bed's clean – you'll probably want to sleep. I'll bring you more food later'.

The warm, dry clothes felt good. The man listened to the rain outside. He didn't want to go back out in it. And besides, if there had been anything on the news, it would be better to hide out until the story had died down. He looked at the woman. She was eccentric maybe, but kind enough to offer him shelter. 'Ok', he said. 'Tomorrow, I move on'. The woman smiled, and when the door closed behind her he was alarmed to hear a key turn in the lock. 'Come on Mr Pepper', she said. 'It's time for your walk'.

When he heard the woman go out he stood up and tried the handle. The door was indeed locked. He looked about the room. It had been someone's bedroom once. He opened the chest of drawers which was full of men's clothes. In the wardrobe hung shirts and suits and a neat row of polished shoes. What had become of the man who'd owned these things? If he'd left surely he'd have taken his clothes too. There were books in the boxes – history books, encyclopaedias and academic literature. Maxim had not gone to university. He'd trained to become a chef and had been lucky enough to get a job in a restaurant when he came to Ireland. His boss, a heavy-set Dublin man, had not been pushed about his lack of papers. He paid him in cash every Friday, telling him with a wink 'not to spend it all in the one shop'. Maxim suspected that it was less than what he'd earn if he were legal, but he had a simple lifestyle and was grateful for the job.

He moved round the room examining the contents of both boxes and drawers. In a desk he came across pictures – holiday snaps of the woman and a dark-haired man. The woman was younger, slimmer – her hair a different shade of blonde. The man had both arms round her holding her in a tight embrace. They looked very much in love. He flicked absently through the photos until he recognised in one of them the blue hoodie she'd given him tied round the man's waist. He stared hard at the picture. There was something about the man's expression that was familiar. And then he realised what it was, he reminded him of his brother, Virgil. What would he think if he knew what had become of him – of how his, Virgil's, actions had led him to this.

Maxim thought about the events of the last month – about how hastily he'd had to leave both the apartment, which he'd been sharing with a couple of students and his job at the restaurant. When his boss heard that the GNIB had launched a major investigation to deport illegal immigrants he'd told him it was too risky to keep him on. He was a decent kind, had given him a bonus with his last payment and said he was sorry to see him go. Only two days later the police had swooped on the apartment and searched his room. The Brazilian guy he shared with had phoned him and told him not to return – the house was being watched. If he was caught he'd be sent back to his country with nothing and that was the last thing he wanted.

Maxim returned the pictures to the drawer. There was nothing else of interest, only bills and letters, some of them addressed to a Mark Roberts and others to a Ms Jacqueline Klein. Ms Klein, it seemed, owed one very large credit card bill according to a bank statement from nearly a year ago. He wondered if she'd paid it or if she had a job. He couldn't see her working in an office, a hairdresser maybe or a beauty therapist, something like that. Maxim was tired. He undressed, pulled back the duvet and crawled beneath it. He would try to sleep until the woman and the dog returned.

It was late in the afternoon when he woke. A sliver of sunlight was creating a prism on the far wall. He was surprised to find himself in the room of boxes. He lay still, listening for any sound of the woman or the dog. His body, voluptuously heavy, was cradled by the mattress, his eyes heavy with sleep. He spent most of the evening slipping in and out of slumber until finally he opened his eyes to find the woman sitting on the end of the bed watching him intently. He sat up with a jolt.

'I didn't mean to startle you'. She put out a hand and then withdrew it again. His heart thudded.

'How long I was asleep?'

'Three or four hours I expect. I looked in when I came back and you were dreaming. Muttering and twitching. I think they must have been bad dreams'.

'Mutter?'

'Speaking … talking in your sleep. Don't worry, I didn't understand any of it. It must have been Moldovan'.

He sat back against the pillows, tried to remember his dreams, but they had fled, no trace remaining.

'Are you hungry?' the woman asked. 'I've been preparing dinner, it'll be ready soon'.

Maxim nodded. He wondered if the woman intended letting him out of the room this time or if she'd bring the food on a tray like before. He listened for a sound of the dog outside.

When the woman left, he got out of bed, pulled on the chinos and the blue hoodie. He sat on the edge of the bed and waited. He wondered if there was a radio. He didn't want to ask, it might arouse her suspicion, but he needed to know if there had been anything on the news. He hoped she wasn't the type who listened to it. Daria never had. The news was always bad, she said. He'd laughed and told her if the world ended she'd be the last to find out. He took it upon himself to tell her what was happening, even if sometimes she refused to listen. She was the type of woman who cried for the misfortune of others. 'I don't know why you think I have to know these things, Maxim', she complained. 'I'd sooner not'.

The door opened and he rose expectantly from the bed. 'Food's ready', the woman said. She turned away from him leaving the door open.

'The dog …'

'Don't worry, I've put him in the bedroom. You don't intend to rob me now, do you?' She smiled. Her lips were full and red. She had changed into a dress of the same colour and a pair of high heels. He followed her into the living room, the dog snuffing beneath the bedroom door as he passed.

He was surprised when he entered the room. Daylight had been shut out by the drawing of a heavy pair of red drapes. On the hearth the woman had scattered a number of tea light candles. Small flames flickered and danced in the grey marble of the fireplace. The effect was one of warmth and if he didn't know better, seduction.

The woman had disappeared into a small annexed kitchen. She returned holding a glass dish between a pair of oven gloves. 'Chicken casserole', she said, and then she hesitated, worried, 'You do eat meat?' Maxim smiled. 'Yes, I eat'. The food was good. He detected a number of spices, rosemary, paprika. The chicken was tender and fell easily from the bone. He nodded his appreciation. 'You cook well', he told her. The woman smiled. 'I enjoy cooking, it relaxes me. And you, what do you like to do?' Maxim spooned some casserole into his mouth, savouring the flavours. 'Same', he said. 'I am chef'.

The woman leaned in, interested. 'Really, is that what you do here in Dublin?'

'I worked in restaurant until few weeks ago. But they have to fire me because of immigration. They don't want any trouble'.

'Ah, I see. And what will you do now?'

Maxim lifted his shoulders in a shrug. 'I don't know, maybe England. If I get enough money, maybe I take the boat'.

'Do you have any family in Moldova that can help you?'

Maxim shook his head. He thought of Virgil and anger stirred inside him. 'I won't ever go back there'.

The woman took a sip of wine. 'Well, maybe you'll have to find a nice Irish girl to marry then', she said, playfully.

As she rose to gather their plates he fought to block an image of Daria in a white lace dress, Virgil by his side as his witness. How long was it before they'd betrayed him, the two people he'd trusted most?

'If you want you could take a shower?' the woman suggested. 'I'll get you a fresh towel. I've washed your clothes so I'm afraid you'll have to use those ones until they dry'.

Maxim looked at the woman and wondered why she was being so nice. 'What's your name?' he asked, pretending he'd not seen it on the bills in the room.

'Did I not to tell you? It's Jackie'.

In the bathroom cabinet Maxim found Lynx deodorant, shaving gel and a number of men's *eau de toilette* sprays. He wondered how recently the man who'd lived here had left and why Jackie hadn't thrown everything out. When Daria had moved out, presumably to stay with Virgil, he'd given her a weekend to clear all her things from their apartment. Anything she'd left he'd dumped. Her dressing gown hanging on the back of the bedroom door was enough to send him into paroxysms.

Maxim ran the water as hot as he could bear it and stepped under the shower. He turned his face up, shampooed his hair and felt himself cleansed of the filth of the outdoors. He thought of the night before, of how his recklessness had led to who knew what kind of disastrous outcome. He would have to leave in the morning before the woman, Jackie, discovered the kind of man she'd given shelter to. But what kind of man was that? Surely no more than a desperate one who'd run out of options.

Above the rush of the water, Maxim thought he heard voices. He stayed still and listened. Suddenly the voices were raised. He turned the water off, afraid to make a sound.

'What the hell are you doing here, Jackie? Just because you still have keys, you have no right …'

He eased the shower door open, took the towel that Jackie had left him and dried himself hurriedly. Clearly, it was the man in the photo, the one who Jackie had claimed was gone. In the bedroom Mr Pepper had started up a racket. 'The fucking dog, Jackie, you've put the fucking dog in the bedroom!'

'What's the problem, Mark? I've been watching the place for you. You should be glad'.

Maxim wished he had his own clothes. He pulled on the clothes that Jackie had given him, wondering if there was any way he could make it out of the apartment without being seen. 'Is there someone else here, Jackie? There is, isn't there? Where is he – in the spare room?' The man passed the bathroom door and swung open the door to the room where Maxim had spent most of the afternoon sleeping. 'Yes, I had someone here, Mark. He's left. What do you care anyway? You made it perfectly clear where we stand'.

They were still in the room. The dog was barking non-stop, hurling itself at the door. Maxim eased the bathroom door open and made a break for it. On the table in the hall the man had left his wallet. Maxim grabbed it and ran for the door. 'Hey, hey you, get back here'. Jackie tried to block the man but he shoved her out of the way. He was tall and moved fast. Maxim had just made it to the stairs when he was grabbed by the hood of the jumper. He tried to turn, swinging his fist at the same time. Just then the dog, who Jackie must have let loose, leaped on the man and both he and Maxim tumbled down the first flight of stairs. The man was howling, cursing and shouting at Jackie to get the damn animal off him. Maxim, who had managed to break free in the tussle, dashed down the stairs and out of the building, door slamming behind him.

He ran until he was sure there was no one following. Then he stopped and looked in the wallet. There was almost three hundred euro – more than enough to buy a boat ticket to England. He took the wad of notes and dropped the wallet in a litter bin. He'd make his way to the port and get the next available ferry.

Maxim boarded a bus for the city centre. He fell into the front seat, shaking still from the fracas. The driver had the radio on and Maxim tensed as the DJ announced the seven o'clock news. He listened to the headlines, understanding most but not all of the words. And then he heard it. 'A man is in a stable condition after the attempted robbery of a service station last night … the robber believed to be a non-national, escaped on foot …' Stable. Maxim tuned out the rest of the woman's words. The man was stable. No damage had been done then – nothing stolen, no one killed. The most he would go down for if they caught him was assault – and all for the sake of a sandwich. Maxim sat back and laid his head against the cool glass of the window. He thought of Jackie Klein and wondered if, from the moment she'd invited him up to the apartment, she'd had a plan to avenge her ex-lover. That, at least, was something he could understand.

By the River's Edge

The fishing trips began when I was ten years old. Daddy and my sister Sarah used to go down to the river and stay there for hours. They'd head down across the field, Daddy carrying the rods and a bag full of tackle, while Sarah skipped by his side with the nets, her blonde ponytail blowing in the breeze. I'd sit outside on the garden gate, swinging to and fro, watching them disappear in the distance. I longed to go with them but Daddy said that I was too young, that I was a nuisance and would only frighten the fish away. I didn't think it was fair. Sarah was only two years older than me, but he insisted and said that when I was older things would be different.

When they were out of sight I'd climb down from the gate and torment our old sheepdog, throwing a burst football which he had no interest in catching. Daddy had had Rowdy since he was a young man. The dog wasn't too fit anymore. He'd wag his tail wanly as I ran up and down the garden path, slapping my thigh and calling for him to run with me. Sometimes he'd follow me but never too far or too quickly. I was bored those afternoons. I wished Daddy had taken me fishing too.

One evening they came home particularly late. I sat by the fire reading and watching the light fade from the evening sky through the living room window. Every so often my mother cast a fretful glance at the clock on the mantle-piece. She leaned forward then and stoked the fire. We both jumped when we heard the back door open. We hadn't seen them come across the fields from the river. I jumped up and ran into the kitchen. Sarah walked straight past me without a word and went up the stairs. Daddy had his foot up on a kitchen chair and was pulling off one of his boots. My mother, who had entered the room behind me, gave him a look as though she were angry.

'Did you catch anything?' I asked.

Daddy shrugged. He put the bucket down. A few silver coloured fish lay in the bottom, but not many. Not like the usual catch. I guessed it hadn't been a good day for fishing.

'Cathy, you go and get ready for bed now like a good girl', my mother said.

She filled the kettle beneath the tap. Her slippers made a soft clip clop on the lino as she moved about the room. My father took his coat off and hung it on the back of the door. He didn't say anything. He just ran his hand through his black beard and sat heavily on one of the wooden chairs.

'Go on now', my mother said.

I crossed the room to give her a goodnight kiss. I put my arms about her waist. She kissed me quickly on the cheek. 'Go on up to bed', she said softly.

'Goodnight, Daddy', I called over my shoulder.

He grunted something in reply. He was in one of his black moods. I skipped into the living room and got my book before going upstairs. Sarah's light was on. She always slept with the light on because she was afraid of the dark. I stuck my head around the door.

'Sarah', I whispered.

She didn't answer. Her head was completely hidden beneath the covers.

'Sarah', I said again.

The form in the bed didn't move. I was surprised that she had fallen asleep so quickly. I crossed the landing to my room. Downstairs, I heard voices. My mother was talking low. My father didn't seem to answer. I went into bed, shut the door and pulled the covers tightly round me. I figured my mother was angry that Daddy and Sarah had come home so late. That was why Sarah had gone straight to bed. That was why she was pretending to be asleep.

Sarah was a light sleeper. Sometimes I crept into bed beside her if I woke in the night and as soon as she heard my foot on the carpet she awoke.

'Sorry', I'd say.

'I wasn't asleep'.

I'd get into bed behind her and snuggle up to her back. She was always warm. I could feel the heat emanate from her skin through her thin cotton nightdress and I'd put my arm around her waist and fall asleep. Sometimes in the night Daddy looked in the door, his huge frame silhouetted against the landing partially lit by a streetlamp whose light crept through a small window that looked down onto our street. When he saw me there he said nothing, just left the room and closed the door softly behind him.

My mother would give out if she found me in Sarah's bed in the morning.

'You have a bed of your own', she'd say.

I could never understand why they didn't want Sarah and me to share a room. Lots of my friends at school shared with their sisters.

'That's because they don't have anywhere else to sleep', my mother said, when I argued. 'We've got this big house and plenty of room for us all'.

At breakfast the next morning Sarah hardly spoke. She played with her cereal, dipping her spoon in the bowl and swirling the milk around until it became a chocolate pool of whirling Coco Pops. Everybody was quiet. My mother cast anxious looks at Sarah, then she looked at my father but he sat there reading the newspaper and didn't look at anyone.

On the way to school Sarah remained quiet. I kicked at the daisies and skipped along by her side. Usually she chatted all the way, about this girl and that boy and who had said what in class. Today she said nothing. She just marched dutifully along and I knew instinctively, just as I did at home, that it was better to say nothing.

'See you later', I said, as we entered the school and headed for our separate classes. I was in fourth class while Sarah was in sixth and was due to make her confirmation that year.

'Yes, see you later', she replied, but she didn't smile and I began to wonder whether I had done something terribly wrong to make everybody so sad.

After school I waited for Sarah. She came out with her two best friends, Melissa and Amy. She seemed in a somewhat brighter mood and waved goodbye as they walked home in the opposite direction. On our way home I told Sarah about a really bold boy who had been put outside the classroom for a whole hour and about the teacher threatening to send a letter home to his parents. She wasn't listening because halfway through my story she interrupted.

'Let's go down to the river', she said.

'We're not allowed to go down to the river, not on our own'.

'Come on, no one will know', she said. 'We'll say we went to a friend's house'.

I was doubtful, but I didn't want to go home without her and so I walked with my sister across the field.

It was a hot afternoon in July. Sarah and I took off our shoes and socks, then sat on the bank and dipped our feet in the water. I closed my eyes and turned my face up to the sun. I could hear the bees humming nearby, collecting nectar to make honey. Daddy had wanted to keep bees last year but my mother said that it was too dangerous and that she wouldn't have them around the place. The heat was strong on my face. When I opened my eyes, I couldn't see for a moment. Then the black spots subsided and I saw Sarah walking close to the water's edge.

'Why is Daddy so angry?' I asked.

Sarah didn't answer for a moment.

'Is it something I've done?' I said.

'No, it's me'.

'Oh'.

I wondered what Sarah could have done. Daddy loved her much more than he loved me. He was always hugging her and taking her places.

Sarah walked with her arms outstretched as though she were on a tightrope.

'What did you do?' I said.

'Nothing'.

I nodded, wondering how that could've made Daddy angry. Sarah stopped walking. She looked at a log that crossed from one side of the river to the other.

'Do you think I could cross that?' she said.

'I don't know, maybe'.

She flipped her blonde ponytail and walked towards the log moving on tiptoe like a ballerina. I watched anxiously as she made her way across the river. Just before she reached the other side she stopped and sat down with one foot on either side of the log, her feet dangling above the water.

'Did you frighten the fish away?' I said.

'What?'

'Yesterday did you frighten the fish away? There weren't very many'.

Sarah looked into the river. She leaned over slightly and trailed her hand in the water.

'We didn't really fish', she said.

'Why not?'

She looked at me hard, her face serious.

'Daddy didn't want to'.

'Then why did you go down to the river?'

My sister's face was hidden by her hair as she continued to lean over, her fingers trailing through the water.

'We fished for a little while but then he said he wanted to play a game'.

'What sort of a game?'

She shrugged. 'I don't know, a grown-up game. He told me not to say anything. He said that you and Mammy would be jealous because he loves me best of all ...'

Sarah leaned further over the water. She tried to catch a piece of stick that was floating towards the log where she sat but the next minute she was in the river and it was carrying her downstream.

'Sarah!'

I screamed my sister's name. She shouted back and tried to swim towards the bank. My sister was a good swimmer but she seemed to be struggling. I didn't know what to do. I wasn't able to swim.

'Come on. Come on', I shouted.

She shouted something back, something about her foot being caught. Then she disappeared from sight. I began to cry. Sarah resurfaced again and shouted at me to go for help. I was torn, standing on the bank watching her and wondering how long it would take me to get to the house.

Then I began to run. I fell on my way across the field and crying I got up and ran again. My mother was in the kitchen when I got there. She ran with me to the river, but when we got there Sarah was gone. For a moment I wondered if she'd managed to get out. If somehow she had got close enough to grab onto one of the branches that hung low over the riverbank.

Sarah's body was found several miles down the river. The water had carried her until the sleeve of her jumper had caught on a branch near the edge and stopped her from going further.

From that day on I didn't speak. My mother tried to talk to me about what happened, but I just looked at her and said nothing. I dreamt about Sarah and in my dreams she was always happy, always laughing. Sometimes I would wake and for that first moment I would think that Sarah was still alive, still sleeping in the room across from mine.

Other times I awoke in the night and thought that I heard Sarah's door opening and I cowered in my bed wondering if she had come back. I lay there in the dark praying that my door wouldn't open, that my sister would not come in and sit on the end of my bed as she sometimes did at night. I was afraid of ghosts and although I loved my sister I didn't want to meet some unearthly version of her wandering in the night.

One night I lay awake in bed. I was cold and desperate to go to the bathroom. It was only two weeks after Sarah had gone and every little noise made my heart knock loudly in my chest. I kept turning in the bed, snuggling under the duvet trying to get warm. I lay there for as long as I could until finally I knew that I would have to go.

I was in the landing returning from the bathroom and congratulating myself on getting there safely when I heard a noise. I stopped and stood quite still, afraid to go any further. The noise appeared to be coming from Sarah's room. It was the sound of someone crying. 'Sarah'. I breathed her name in the dark, terrified at the prospect of seeing her. Yet curiosity prevented me from moving. As I stood there and listened the crying stopped. I was about to return to my room when the door of Sarah's room opened. Terrified, I stepped back but it was not Sarah who stood in the doorway. It was my mother. She was in her dressing gown and her eyes were all red from crying.

'Cathy. What are you doing out here?' she said.

She wiped her eyes hurriedly and tightened the belt of her dressing gown.

I didn't say anything, just stood there and stared at her as though she were an apparition.

'Go on now like a good girl and go back to bed', she said.

She put her arm around my shoulder and ushered me back towards my room. I turned and hugged her tightly, pulling her down towards me. Her body was warm and I didn't want to let her go but she straightened up and kissed me on the head.

'See you in the morning love', she said.

Before I closed my bedroom door I saw her go downstairs. I wondered why she didn't go to bed but maybe, like me, she couldn't sleep. It was the first time that I heard my mother crying. After that I often heard Sarah's door opening and closing at night. I think my mother slept in that room, amongst Sarah's things.

Everything was different when Sarah was gone. The house was quiet. My mother and father seemed hardly to speak. Sometimes I looked up from doing my homework and he was staring at me over his newspaper. I was frightened of my father then, of his black looks and silences. Other times he disappeared for days. My mother seemed more relaxed then. She would talk to me as she worked and I would listen and feel almost happy.

A few days later, after my father returned, darkness would descend over the house. His presence affected everything, contaminated all that was good. I usually kept out of his way. I would play in my room, or if my mother permitted it I would play outside in the garden. She had become very protective since Sarah had gone but I had no urge to wander too far anyway, not without my sister.

I was playing in the living room one day while my mother made the dinner when my father appeared in the room with the fishing rods.

'Come on. We're going fishing', he said.

I looked up from my place on the floor but didn't say anything. I didn't want to go fishing, not since Sarah had told me about the game they had played and how I imagined she hadn't like it.

My father crossed the room. He threw the fishing rods down against one of the armchairs and pulled me roughly by the arm.

'I said come on'.

I stood up, shakily. His arm was under my elbow. I wanted to tell him to stop, that I didn't want to go fishing but I hadn't spoken since Sarah had died and I wasn't sure that I knew how to anymore.

He was picking up the rods again and ushering me towards the door when my mother came into the room.

'You're not taking her anywhere', she said.

Her voice trembled with anger. My father looked at her but said nothing.

'Sarah. Come here', she said.

I wanted to correct her mistake, to tell her that I was Cathy, not Sarah. Instead, I simply ran to her and she put her hands on my shoulders.

My father stood in the door looking at her in surprise.

'I want you to leave', she said. 'I can't stand living in the same house as you anymore. I don't even want to look at you'.

He tried to protest, but she didn't let him finish. I stood there, frightened, wondering what he might do next. My mother tightened her grip on my shoulders so that her fingers were almost biting into my flesh but I knew that she meant me no harm.

'I know what you did', she said.

I watched as my father's face grew pale. He clutched the rods, not knowing whether to come or go.

Eventually he went upstairs. We could hear him banging about in the rooms. We stood in the living room, my mother and I, saying nothing, doing nothing. We remained like that until he re-appeared with a bag in his hand. He stopped in front of my mother as though he were about to say something. I was afraid he might hit her, but he left without another word. We heard the car start, then the crunch of the tyres on the gravel drive. My mother held me, her body shaking. And I cried for the first time since my sister had died.

Parting Shot

'You're late', she said. Luiza Sadowski was sitting, hands cupped round a large white mug glaring at me. She put the mug down and pulled at a stray thread hanging from one pink-striped, fingerless glove. I began to laugh, her abruptness had become so predictable.

'Two more minutes and I'd have left', she stated. Her nails, metallic gold, tapped a tuneless rhythm on the wooden bench before her.

'Tell you what', I said. 'Let's not bother, shall we? I'll meet you another day when you're in a better mood'.

She made a sweeping gesture with one gloved hand, just missing her coffee mug. 'No, no, you're here now. Get something'.

We were sitting in the outdoor section of the cafe. I was less than ten minutes late and, what's more, had texted to say that I would be. Now, I ordered a coffee from the waitress and shivered. 'Jesus, Sadowski, you would have to get a table outside, wouldn't you? Does that mean you're back on the cigarettes?'

Even as I said it, she was rummaging in her bag. She took out a cigarette skin and began to line it with tobacco. 'I wouldn't if I hadn't been driven to it'. Meticulously, she sprinkled and spread the tobacco before tonguing the paper and tamping it shut.

'How *is* Kev?'

She tossed her head in annoyance, flicked her lighter and inhaled on the cigarette. 'He's such a fucking mummy's boy'. Her words spewed in a haze of smoke as she exhaled through one corner of her red mouth. 'Just because she's on chemo it doesn't mean he has to be at her beck and fucking call'.

A pulse kicked off in my head. My own mother had died of cancer the previous year and I still had constant nightmares about it. 'Nice', I said. 'I suppose you said that about me too?'

Her hand went to her mouth and she leaned forward to take my hand. 'I'm so sorry', she said, 'I didn't think. It's just, he really winds me up you know?'

The waitress arrived with my coffee, giving me the opportunity to take my hand back. Luiza didn't get family bonds. She'd had a turbulent relationship with both her parents. She had a brother, too, who didn't speak to her. She'd never told me why, but I had a good idea it had something to do with some caustic remark she'd made about his wife. I know she didn't like her. In the six years Luiza had lived in Dublin there'd been no contact between them.

'I don't know why you don't just finish it. You never have anything good to say about him. And to be frank, I don't know how he puts up with you'.

'Well, why do you', she shot back, 'if I'm such a horrible person?' Her green eyes teared up, threatening to smear the perfect black line around them. That was the thing about Luiza, she was soft beneath the spikes. There was no way I'd have stayed friends with her otherwise.

She recovered seconds later, crushed her cigarette and sat back in her chair. 'You know what? You're much more tolerable since Lenny broke up with you. You're not super-happy all the time making the rest of us feel like crap'.

'Thanks Luiza. And there I was thinking you'd been my saviour out of kindness, stupid of me not to realise you were basking in my misery. You're some bitch sometimes, you know that?' I stood to leave.

She stood too. 'Ah look, that's not what I meant … it's just you're always so bloody positive, it's hard to deal with sometimes. Here, I forgot to give you this'. She picked up a paper bag that had been next to her on the table.

'What is it?'

'Muffins. I baked them for you last night'.

'Muffins? What did you put in them, arsenic? Tell you what, Luiza, you can keep your muffins – and what's more, I hope Kev grows a backbone one of these days, walks out and keeps on walking. You don't bloody deserve him'.

I threw the price of my coffee on the table and marched out leaving Luiza Sadowski staring after me.

It was about a week later, close to midnight, when she rang. Had it been daylight I'd probably not have answered but the ringtone dragging me from sleep caught me somewhat unaware. 'Hello?' My greeting was met by an unintelligible litany of sounds. 'Luiza?' The relentless blubbing continued. Wide awake now I threw back the covers and turned on the light.

'Ssh, calm down. I'm listening'.

Finally, the braying subsided. 'He's gone', she said. 'Won't answer his phone either. What am I going to do?'

'Ssh, look – where are you?'

'His place. I came over to talk to him but he won't open the door. There's a car in the driveway too. Maybe, maybe he's in there with someone else'.

'Christ, Luiza, do me a favour and get out of there. With any luck he's out and won't know you've been. Come over and we'll figure it out'.

More trembling breaths. 'But what if there's someone in there … what if she's …'

'It's probably nothing, a friend's car or his sister's … look just get over here. You don't want to look like a stalker'.

I got out of bed, pulled my dressing gown on and turned on the heat. It looked to be a long night. Jesus, Sadowski, it would happen on a weeknight, wouldn't it? Still, despite her attitude and our recent row, I owed her one – and I did feel slightly guilty that my parting shot had come to fruition.

I walked round the living room tidying up, thinking of my own predicament nearly a year before when everything had come to a head with Lenny. It was Luiza who had told me, Luiza who had stopped me from making a complete fool of myself and in the aftermath she was the one who had sat up nights and listened to my constant bleating.

Lenny, who used to call me three times a day, simply disappeared for a whole weekend. It had started with a cancelled date on the Friday, a migraine attack he'd said. When I called him the next day he didn't answer. Sunday came and the silence remained unbroken. I was crazy thinking that something had happened to him.

It was a phone call from Luiza a few days later that revealed the reality. Lenny had uploaded his profile on a dating site she'd signed up to. She phoned me straight away when she saw it. I said it must have been an old profile, he'd told me about his internet dating disasters before we'd started going out. 'Cath – it says he was online five minutes ago. His picture is the one from your birthday party. He's cut you out of it. I can see your arm around him. It's definitely yours, I recognise your silver bracelet'. I'd got in the car and gone straight over to confront him. He said it wasn't on, 'doorstepping' him like that. We had a shouting match and he said that Luiza was a bloody liar. Toxic was what he called her. He got that bit right.

The buzzer went and I let Luiza Sadowski in. Her eyes were all puffy from crying, her newly-cropped black hair made her face look even paler than usual. 'What happened?' I asked. She was more mad than weepy now. 'We had an argument. I told him if he answered the phone to his mother one more time, I mean, she rings every time we're in bed. I swear it's like she knows and of course mummy's boy has to answer'.

I said nothing. It was going to be hard to support Luiza, not when I was silently cheering Kevin on. 'So what did he do?'

'Nothing. Can you believe it? He said nothing. Just walked out and slammed the door, that was two days ago'.

'Look, it's probably for the best. You told me yourself how much he winds you up'.

She leaned in, cat's eyes narrowed. 'But you don't get it, he ended it! He doesn't get to end it, I do'.

The week passed and Luiza heard nothing from Kev. She'd texted him umpteen times and called him as many. 'Maybe he's lost his phone', I told her. She glared at me. 'He hasn't amnesia', she said. 'He knows where I live'.

By Saturday she'd become frantic. I'd brought her out for a drink hoping to take her mind off things, but she obsessed all night. At around midnight she looked at her watch. 'Right, I can't take any more of this', she said. 'I have to find out what's going on'.

'And how do you propose to do that?' I asked her.

'Let's go over there'.

'Luiza you can't, you've done it before, it didn't do you any ...'

'I'm not going to knock. It's Friday, he won't get home till after one. You forget I know his routine, so we're going to watch the house, see if he comes home alone or not'.

'Luiza, come on, that's stalking, it's just ... it's unhealthy'.

'Think of it more as a stakeout. You know I won't be satisfied until I find out if he's met someone. If he has, then that's it. I'll let him get on with it'. She grinned. 'Right after I've keyed his nice shiny Skoda'.

'He'll recognise the car'.

'Ah, but he won't because we'll take yours instead. You haven't been drinking'.

Kev lived in a three-bedroom house, the value of which had plummeted in the crash leaving him in negative equity. It was in the middle of a long block of identical houses and I had to slow down so that Luiza could point out the right one.

'Now what?' I said.

'Park on the opposite side', she said, 'not this close, but somewhere we can still see'.

I parked outside a house with a high garden hedge but I felt twitchy. Whoever lived there could see us clearly from the upstairs windows.

'How long are we going to sit here?'

'Just until we see him go in. He'll get a taxi, he always takes a taxi home on a Friday night'.

A light went on in the house we'd parked outside. I saw the slats of the blind pulled apart as someone looked out. 'What if they come out and ask us what we're doing here?' I said.

'Sssh, here's a taxi now'. We watched as the cab slowed at the bend and then passed, taxi plate unlit. Not him. My bladder was beginning to ache. 'Luiza ...'

'Can't believe I ever went with him to begin with', she said. She rummaged in her bag, pulled out her tobacco and began to roll a cigarette. 'Not in the car, Luiza'. She glanced round. 'Won't make any difference', she said, eyeing the rubbish strewn on the floor. 'There are new life forms growing in here, Cath'. She finished rolling but didn't light up.

'At least Lenny was good-looking', she said. 'But Kev ... Did you ever hear from him after?'

'Lenny? No. Not so much as a text'.

'Hmph. What was it you two fought about anyway?'

'What do you mean ... the disappearing act, the dating site, remember?'

Luiza frowned. 'Oh yeah'.

'What do you mean "oh yeah". You were the one who told me about it'.

She looked at the cigarette between her fingers, clicked the lighter and waved it near the tip, the cigarette smoked but didn't catch. She placed it between her lips.

'Luiza ...'

'Sssh, maybe this is it'. The dazzle of headlights as a car rounded the bend. Instinctively, we shrank in our seats, but again the car failed to slow – and disappeared, red taillights fading like embers into the night.

'Luiza, you did see Lenny's profile on that site, right?'

She shrugged. 'You were obsessing over him. Had to tell you something, didn't I? I couldn't listen to it anymore night after night after night'.

I didn't think about what I was doing. I made a lunge and grabbed Luiza's bag from her lap. She screamed and covered her face with her hands thinking I was going to attack her. I leant across, flung open the door and roared at her to get out. As I did so, I hurled the bag as hard as I could and Luiza, in shock, staggered after it. She was on her knees, cigarette bent comically in her mouth, chasing the contents of the bag, when the next car came round the bend. I flashed my lights as a warning and then leaned on the horn, but the driver didn't heed me. He said the last thing he saw before he knocked her clear was Luiza Sadowski's widened eyes caught in the glare of the headlights.

Counting Stars

Bart awoke in a box room, with nursery-rhyme paper on the walls and tried to stretch in a four-foot bed, much too small for his large frame. He lay there and looked at his bare feet sticking out from beneath the covers. Today he was fifty years old.

Downstairs he heard the radio playing. Alice was making breakfast. The high-pitched voice of his granddaughter penetrated the ceiling, accompanied by the baby's shrill cry. The clatter of dishes added to the cacophony of sound. Soon she would come upstairs and poke her head around the door to see if he was awake. If he kept his eyes closed she would leave the tray on the locker by the bed. For the past few days he ate nothing. Food was like cotton wool in his mouth. He tried to chew, but when he swallowed it felt as though it stuck in his throat. It then lodged in his gut, undigested.

The kitchen door opened and the voices were amplified.

'Let me, Mammy, let me'.

'No, Ruby. It's too heavy, you wouldn't be able to carry it'.

Bart closed his eyes. He heard them coming up the stairs, the dishes rattled on the tray. He pulled the covers up to his chin. The door creaked open. He felt the little girl standing over him. Her shallow breath fanned his skin.

'Granddad', she said.

Alice put the tray down and shook him gently. 'Come on, Dad, you have to eat'.

Bart opened his eyes, stretched and then rubbed at his eyes as though he had been asleep.

'Happy Birthday, Granddad'. The child leaned over and looped her arms around his neck crushing herself to him.

Bart blinked away the tears that threatened to overwhelm him. He looked at the child, then he looked at his daughter. He remembered her in her high chair, throwing the spoon at him when he tried to feed her. Now it was his turn to refuse to eat. He sat up in bed, smiled forcibly at the little girl and pinched her cheek.

'Thanks pet', he said, taking the tray from the locker, though the sight of the food made his stomach contract.

Alice was like her mother. She had the same profile, the same heart-shaped face and brown eyes. Her hair fell softly around her shoulders and swayed as she moved. He remembered the smell of Claire's hair. He had liked to hold her close to him and inhale her scent. He would rub his face in her tresses and she would laugh and say that he was crazy. Crazy. It was a word that she had used frequently in the last few days. He felt like he was going crazy. Every morning he wanted to pinch himself to see if it was real. Yesterday it took him a minute or two to remember. When he did he wanted to fall back asleep again to try to forget. He had this sick feeling in the pit of his stomach that would not subside. It was the same feeling he got years ago, when he went to meet her, but as soon as he saw her he forgot. She could make him forget anything back then.

Last night he went downstairs, he brought a blanket with him and curled up on the sofa. He needed to get out of bed, to get out of that room. He didn't know where to put himself to stop the pain. How can you escape from something that's deep within you? He got cold and went back upstairs. Besides, he didn't want them to find him there in the morning. He couldn't stand their pitying stares. His daughter was good to him. She was brusque, but in a gentle way. His son-in-law invited him to the pub. 'Come on, Bart', he said, 'come down and watch the match. England are sure to go down today'. Bart refused politely. He could have gone and sat there and drank himself into oblivion. He could have allowed the noise and the crowd to overwhelm him. There was no man who liked better the football and the crowd, but not this time, nothing would quell this sick feeling and so he stayed at home.

Home. That was another word that crushed him. He had not been home in several days. He had gone over to the house and she had come out to the car but she didn't invite him in. It angered him to think that he had to be invited into his own home. He'd sat outside and watched the windows, wondering if there was anyone else in the house – whether *he* was there, sitting in Bart's chair, watching his television, talking to his wife. She hadn't said much. What was there for her to say? She didn't apologise. Not that he wanted her to, but it bothered him that she seemed to think that she had done nothing wrong.

'We were separated', she said.

It was true. They had been living apart for three months, but he never thought it would come to this. Separation had meant nothing before. They always got back together. But this, he guessed, was one separation too many. This time she had met someone new. They sat there in the car and she refused to talk. She was shrewd, Claire. She didn't want to say anything that might implicate herself – that might make her look like she was in the wrong for a change. He asked her questions. Was it serious? How long had it been going on? She avoided answers. Told him she didn't know, that it had only been a couple of months, who knows where it might or might not go? He knew that there was more to it than that – you don't throw away thirty years of marriage on a whim.

Bart lay in bed and looked at the ceiling. Above him glow-in-the-dark stars dulled with daylight. At night, he lay there sleepless. The stars shone brightly over his head and he thought about his future. She met him at a wedding, this man. He knew him vaguely to see, knew that he was a fly-by-night, someone who never stayed in the one place too long. He was just her type. She, the bohemian girl, who didn't want to get married, but found herself pregnant at the age of nineteen. Did she resent him for it? Perhaps. She never said that she did but that was Claire all over. She wouldn't say such things, she didn't like to hurt people's feelings. They had their other children in quick succession, a boy and then another girl. They were parents of three at twenty-three years old – too young for a family.

The first time she left him was her thirtieth birthday. He'd come home drunk. He had promised to take her out for dinner, but got held up with the boys. 'Just the one, Bart', they had said as they lured him to the pub after work. Just the one. He never had just the one though. She was sitting there wearing a red dress. She had put her hair up and soft tendrils fell about her shoulders. She'd sent the baby-sitter home. 'Happy birthday', he said. Even through the haze he knew that he was wrong and she was so damn beautiful. She didn't reply. She simply stood up and crossed the room. She brushed past him on her way to the door. Her perfume lingered in the room when she was gone. He slumped in the chair and asked himself why he was such an idiot? A week later he coaxed her into coming home.

Bart lay there and began to count the stars, willing sleep. Why hadn't he tried harder, drank less, spent more time with her, listened to what she wanted? The stars blurred, but his thoughts raged on. They had drifted through the years, row after row, separation after separation. Now it had come to this, a chance meeting at a wedding, a wedding with his name on the invitation card which he'd chosen not to attend. It was driving him crazy. He thought about that man's hands on her body, the body that he had known inside out, that he had slept next to for all those years. It was difficult to think of her with another man. He thought again of the conversation they had in the car. 'Was it serious?' he'd asked. Christ, she was forty-nine years old, he knew they weren't simply holding hands. She wouldn't tell him, wouldn't let anything slip. He wanted to know, even if knowing made him feel like shit. He'd prefer the truth than the wild ramblings of his imagination.

The first thing he did when he woke up every morning was pick up the phone and call her. She tried to make out that he was crazy, that he was stalking her, but all he wanted was the truth. All he wanted was to talk to his wife. She was abrupt, she didn't want to talk to him, she didn't want to argue. She'd had enough of arguing. She'd had over thirty years. He hung up the phone, dismal. He wondered whether she was alone or whether he was there with her, the wedding guy or her sister. He knew her sister would be happy, she had never liked him. He knew it by the way she spoke to him, by the way her face changed when he walked into a room. She figured he wasn't good enough for Claire. He figured he wasn't good enough for Claire but somehow he'd struck lucky. She loved him for more years perhaps than he deserved. How many more years could she have put up with – thirty more? And that was the worst part – that was the thing that hurt like hell, he couldn't blame her. Sure he could blame her, he could hate her for finding someone else, but he knew that he only had himself to blame and that was the part that he could not escape. The reason that made him get up in the night and wander the house looking for some place to escape to, but he could not escape himself. That was the crux.

Downstairs the television came on. Music seeped through the ceiling. Cartoons. He knew the high-pitched voices, he had watched them enough with his own children. At least he was a good dad. His children were all grown now. He'd been living with Alice since the separation but he knew that he couldn't stay. He didn't want to impose, he was too old for this.

Bart raised himself on one elbow, he blinked and the stars came right. He must get the house valued. It was clear that this time it was over, this time Claire could not forgive him. There had been too much water under the bridge. He sat upright and looked out the window. A 'For Sale' sign loomed in a garden across the way. It would be a lot of upheaval. He could either try to buy her out or sell up and move away. Either way it would cost him. He had never imagined having to get out a mortgage at this time of his life. And Claire, what would she do? The wedding guy, he had nothing to his name – he knew that. Perhaps they would travel together, leave this place and follow her girlhood dream now that their children were grown. Bart pinched himself. It didn't hurt but it was real. Tomorrow was real and the day after that. Slowly he got dressed. He would phone the real estate agents. He couldn't sleep another night in that bed.

THE PICNIC

'Turn it up, Connie, this is an awesome song'.

Awesome – there's something about that word that irks me more than it should. Mandy's leaning on the back of my seat, her breath on my neck, her faux Americanisms in my left ear. She starts to sing – a warbling nasal trill. In truth Mandy's not a bad singer as long as she doesn't morph into Britney Spears. That's the thing about Mandy – she's a chameleon, constantly shifting to become something other than what she is.

'Give a little respect, to-o-o-o me'. She bounces between us, one hand on the back of Maja's seat and the other on mine.

'Jesus, Mandy, would you ever quit it. I'm trying to drive here'.

The bouncing stops. She sits back, humming now and refuses to meet my eye in the rear view mirror, staring out the window through her tangled red hair.

'How long has Sine to stay in this place?' Maja asks, suddenly.

'Till she gets her marbles back, I suppose', Mandy pipes up. I swear I'm one comment from grinding the car to a stop and abandoning her to the Wicklow hills. Maja ignores Mandy and looks at me, my hands tight on the wheel. 'Until she feels she can face it, I guess'. Even as I say the words, I'm not sure what *it* is – life, her parents or what it was this time that drove Sine to seek shelter in the big house on four acres where they said you could salve brittle nerves.

A week before I had driven out here alone. Sine had transferred from St John of God's to this impressive country home. She was not ready for discharge but no longer was she a danger to herself. Respite was what she needed, a quiet place to recover. The carers were friendly, they'd smiled at Sine and said she was doing well. It might be nice, they'd told me, if some of her friends wanted to come up and take her out for the day. And so here we were, Mandy, Maja and me driving out to Aughrim to take Sine on a picnic.

'Wow, nice place', Maja says, as we pull up in front of the large stone house. 'It must be very old'. Maja is into buildings. In Poland she'd studied to be an architect but then she'd come here and started teaching EFL like me. She loves teaching but lately she's been threatening to return to Poland and to her profession. She feels guilty, she says, being away from her family for so long. It's breaking her mother's heart.

'Well, no bars on the windows, that's a good sign', Mandy says.

'I swear to God ...' I mutter and Maja gives me a look that tells me to leave it. Mandy is Sine's friend, too, no matter what I might think of her.

Sine is up and sitting cross-legged on the bed writing when we get to her room. She throws the notebook down and jumps up happily. 'Hey you lot. Glad to see you didn't kill each other on the way down here'. She's wearing white cut-off jeans and a pale pink top that hangs off one shoulder. There's mischief in her eyes that I haven't seen in a while. 'Well, look at you', Maja says, 'you look fantastic'. I strain to see what Sine's been writing in the red notebook while Maja gives her a hug.

'Are you working on a new story?' I ask.

Sine smiles. 'An idea came to me, it might be nothing, but I'm giving it a try. Now are you lot breaking me out of here or what?'

Mandy grins and links Sine down the corridor and out into the warmth of July.

We drive to the ruins of an old abbey. There's a car park and we pull in and unload the boot. Mandy takes the picnic basket while I take out my guitar case and a flask of tea. 'How are the folk sessions going?' Sine asks me. I pull a face. 'They're not! I finally had enough of cancelled gigs and Gary's selective amnesia when it came to getting paid'. Sine looks at me, serious. 'That's too bad. I thought you really liked it'. 'I did, but you can't stick around and be someone's fool either. Sure, it's not all bad, he taught me a few chords. Let him go and find a new singer'.

We spread the blanket in the grass and Maja takes the food out. She's brought chicken drumsticks, cold meat, coleslaw, humus, a veritable salad feast. 'And Polish cheesecake for dessert', she announces, uncovering the dish like a magician. 'What flavour is it?' I ask. 'Natural', she says. 'Oh', I say, not exactly liking the sound of cheese-flavoured cheesecake.

Mandy gnaws at a drumstick and dips it in the humus. 'They were all asking for you at Toastmasters', she tells Sine. 'Oh, yeah. What did you tell them?' Sine asks, her head lowered, expression hidden beneath a floppy straw sun hat. Mandy shrugs. 'Nothing, just that you were away'. I finish eating and push my plate away.

'Toastmasters is a great concept', I say, 'I can see why you'd do it, Sine. It must help a lot with your readings, but is it not full of egoists, people who love the sound of their own voices?' Mandy doesn't get the dig. 'There are all sorts there', she says, tearing at the drumstick and talking with her mouth full. 'A lot of corporate types and yeah, a few just looking for an audience'. I look at her and wonder how she and Sine became friends.

I lie back in the grass and feel the sun on my face. Maja messes around with my guitar, picking an arpeggio that she learned as a teenager, trying to remember how to play. 'What's your new story about, Sine?' she asks. I turn slightly to look at Sine, shading my eyes with my hand. She's picking at the grass, the brim of her hat hiding her face in shadow.

'It's about two friends', she says. 'They're out in a club one night and they meet these two blokes'.

Mandy guffaws. 'Sounds familiar. Coco's on a Saturday night, eh? Awesome!'

Sine ignores her. 'One of the girls is really into the guy she meets, her friend isn't into the other one, he's a bit strange, doesn't meet her eyes when she's talking to him. But she puts up with him anyway for her friend's sake, and he keeps buying her drinks until she's palatic. By that time she's just talking shite and has forgotten the fact that she doesn't even like him. When the club's over, Shelley – that's the girl's name – doesn't see her friend. She's not feeling too well at this stage and the bloke helps her outside. Her friend, Carol, is standing up against a wall snogging the other fella who, Shelley has to admit, is very good-looking. He has a nice way of speaking, too. He has a fancy car, a black Volvo and he offers Carol and Shelly a lift home'.

Sine pauses and stares out over the fields. 'Sine', I say, but it's like she doesn't hear me. 'Carol gets in the front next to the good-looking one. Shelley can see he has his hand on her leg. She leans forward between the seats. "Hey, this isn't the right way", she tells them. Carol tells her they're going up to the viewing point. "It's beautiful, Shell", she says, "you can see all the lights of the city". Shelley feels sick'.

Sine's on a roll now, she's forgotten her audience. I sit up, hug my knees and cast my mind back to that night, the night I got off with that Tony in Coco's club. He hadn't called after. I was so pissed off – I thought he was a decent guy. He'd seemed interested. Maja is looking at Sine, rapt. Not even Mandy interrupts to break the spell. An uneasy feeling comes over me as Sine goes on. We'd been so drunk that night, but it had been a laugh, hadn't it?

'They get up to the car park, the viewing point as Carol calls it. It's up past Killakee, at the foot of the Hell Fire Club. Carol and your man get out of the car – say they're going for a walk. Shelley's had to get out of the car too at this point, to puke. The one in the back says he'll stay with her, make sure she's alright. Carol tells her she'll be grand once she gets it all out of her system. Shelley hears them laughing in the dark as they disappear up the hill behind the car park. It's ok for a while. Your man stands there smoking, looking at the lights. Shelley doesn't feel as bad, her head's stopped spinning. "I don't usually drink so much", she tells the guy. She doesn't even know what his name is. It's cold, so they get back in the car. Shelley looks to see if the other bloke, the good-looking one, has left the key in. They might be able to listen to the radio, but he's taken it with him. Your man puts his arm around her, leans in and starts kissing her, aggressive like, all tongue. Shelley pulls away from him, tells him she's not interested – but he's strong. "What did you come up here for then, you little bitch?" he says'.

I'm looking at Sine, tears stinging my eyes. I want her to stop and I want her to go on. Me and Tony, the walk up to the Hell Fire Club. He kissed me – that was it. What was it had gone on back there? Jesus, Sine.

'By the time the other two got back it was over. Shelley couldn't look at your man. He was jittery now, smoking one cigarette after the other. "You're alright", he said. Was she? Was she alright? Carol and your man were all loved up. He was gentle with her, spoke nice. "Jesus, not in the car, Alec", he told your man when he lit up. Was that his name, Alec?'

Sine turns to me when she says this. 'The next day they said it was a right laugh. And Shelley said she'd never get that drunk again. Carol said she'd made a show of herself alright, nearly getting sick in that Tony's nice car. Shelley said nothing else, pretended everything was alright. She figured she must've led your man on, done something to make him think she was up for it'. Sine stopped and pulled at a strand of grass.

'Well, I hope she never spoke to that Carol again', Mandy snorted. 'Imagine leaving her there with that monster'.

When I look up, Maja is watching me, her grey eyes full of truth. She stands and starts to clear away the used picnic things. 'Come on, Mandy, give me a hand', she says. Mandy looks up, uncomprehendingly. She's propped on her elbows, legs stretched before her. 'But I want to hear the end of Sine's story', she says.

Sine shrugs. 'There is no end. I'm still working it out in my head'.

Maja takes the picnic basket and Mandy lopes after her. Sine and I take two corners of the blanket each and our hands and eyes meet. 'Jesus, Sine, why didn't you tell me?' Sine looks away. 'It happened, that's all'.

'But if we hadn't gone up there, if I hadn't agreed to take that lift ...'

Ahead of us Mandy has stopped walking. She's turned back and is squinting into the sun. She shakes her head and shouts across to us. 'God, that Carol was some bitch. I mean what kind of person would do that?' But she's no longer looking at Sine. Her eyes are on me alone.

Mise-en-Scene

'So you'll never guess what?'

'Probably not', I say as I lounge back in a beanbag in Accents cafe. It's our new hangout since Izzy did an improv show here. Personally, I don't care for the basement of anywhere, no matter how hip and funky. I like windows, big windows where my mind can drift, up and out, drawn by the world outside.

'Pablo's on Plenty of Fish again'. Mel sits back, eyes narrowed. Three faces turn towards mine, waiting for my reaction.

'Nothing to stop him, is there?' I say. 'It *is* three months ago since we split up'.

Pablo. Or Paul to be exact. Mel had called him Pablo from the start. If she hadn't, none of it would have happened.

'Do you mean to say you're over him?' she asks, arching one burgundy-tinted brow.

I shrug. 'He's entitled to do what he likes, isn't he? None of my business anymore'. I'm about to add, 'sure he could even date you, Mel', but that would be throwing oil on a blaze. It's better to let her think I'm over it, over the whole freaking fiasco.

Only Anja knows how much I'm not over it. She comes to the rescue now by steering the conversation on a different course. 'How's the eBay business going, Mel?'

Mel shakes her head. 'I've packed it in. Nothing was shifting. I meant to say actually, I've a load of clothes in the apartment, Izzy. You should come over and have a look. They're big sizes – 18'.

Izzy looks up from her iphone. 'What! Do you think I'm an 18? Seriously?'

Mel shrugs. 'What's wrong with 18 – sure, I'm a 16 depending on the store. It's called ample cleavage. Nothing to be ashamed of', she smirks.

Izzy stands. 'Well, I'll tell you what you can do, Mel. You can stick your size 18 up your ...'

'Cappuccino?' The waitress appears at my elbow as Izzy storms in the direction of the toilets, phone in hand.

'Jesus', Mel says, 'what's eating her?'

Pablo. Paul. He said he'd never go back on that site no matter what happened – but then it wasn't exactly a surprise. People said all sorts of things they didn't mean and he hadn't turned out to be the exception.

'Didn't think you were going back on that site either, Mel', I say. 'Didn't you say it was full of perverts and losers?'

Mel grins. 'The first I've learned to live with', she says. 'Sometimes certain needs prevail'.

'Have you been on any dates recently?' Anja asks, reaching for her chai latte. She's into herbal everything since she returned from her trip to India. She's even had her nose pierced, a tiny diamond that twinkles each time she turns her head.

'Not sure I'd call them dates exactly, but there's this chef, has been over to my place a couple of times ...'

'Oh yeah? Are you going out?'

Mel leans in, conspiratorially, plum-coloured fringe, newly dyed, falling in her eyes. 'We don't go out, Anja', she says. 'We stay in. Here wait till I show you his pic, you've got to see this'. She rummages in her oversized bag for her phone, thumbs an app and hands the phone to Anja. 'Jesus Christ!' Anja says, 'Are you serious, Mel?' She passes the phone to me.

Mel spreads her hands dramatically. 'Behold, the naked chef!' she says.

A selfie – phone in his hand – taken in his bathroom. I can see white tiles and a blue shower curtain behind him, but the background isn't exactly the focal point. The chef is ripped, a solid six-pack a la Matthew McConaughey, biceps swollen, skin tanned. The picture borders on the pornographic, a tight pair of navy CK shorts pulled low over his groin. The face, well, the face isn't great – thinning hair, a beaked nose, eyes set too close together.

At that moment Izzy returns and leans in over my shoulder to see what all the hysteria is about. 'Who's the prawn?' she says. I can't hold in the laughter. 'Prawn?' I repeat. 'Yeah, great body, pity about the head'.

Mel stands and snatches the phone back.

'Where's he from?' I ask.

'Cabra'.

'Jesus, I figured he was from South America. Where did he get a colour like that, this Cabra chef? He must live in a stand-up tanning booth!'

I sip at my coffee and pretend to be interested in Mel's sex life, but all I can think of is Paul back on that site – back looking.

We say goodbye outside the cafe, it's falling dark and Mel seems in a great hurry to get going. If she has a liaison with the chef she doesn't say. Not after the ribbing we've given her. She strides away, leaving Iz and me standing. Anja has already left, mumbling something about a ukulele class.

'Iz, she didn't mean it', I say softly. 'You know what she's like, zero tact'.

'She's a cow is what she is – size bloody 18 – I'm telling you, I'm seriously thinking of culling the company I keep'.

I nod, usually we laugh about Mel and her blunt ways, but lately she's becoming more and more toxic. At first I figured it was only with me, because of what happened, but the girls say no, that Mel has simply become worse. She doesn't care what she says or who she hurts with her words. It's the reason my guilt's abated. Mel, on a good day, doesn't exactly inspire sympathy. But wait, I haven't even told you what happened yet.

Rewind ten months. Mel standing outside the Olympia, tugging on a cigarette. Red beret angled on her then jet black thatch. Lips coated siren red. Her Betty Boop phase. Distance has made it a film reel, I play it back, observe all our reactions. Paul and me, arms round each other, on our way to see a Doors tribute band – his first time to meet my friends. Mel. Her hand falters, she smacks her red lips together, draws on the cigarette and exhales through the side of her mouth. 'Well, if it isn't Pablo', she says. Her eyes, cobalt blue, between the fake black lashes, flint-like – his face turning a shade not dissimilar to her blazing mouth. I had no need to ask how they'd met.

She said she was ok with me seeing him. She managed to rewrite the story of what had happened and I wondered if she'd forgotten telling us that he'd stopped calling, stopped texting, simply faded off the planet after a few weeks of them dating. In the redraft Pablo had been a bore.

Good looking, yeah, but he hadn't been her type. She wanted someone funkier, a drummer or something, not some corporate type living in a semi-D, but we both knew there was more to Paul than that.

I spend half the night searching for Paul's profile. First I enter his handle PAC33 – Paul Anthony Conlon, 33 for his age, but nothing shows. I figure he's set up a new profile, knowing that I'd check. I click advanced search and enter his details. Starsign: Libra. Eyes: blue. Height 5'8–5'10. Nothing. Has he been shrewd enough to change some of the details? Two hours later having trawled through several hundred profiles, I reach the end. No Paul. What was Mel talking about? She'd specifically said Plenty of Fish, but maybe she got it wrong, maybe it was some other website. I come across the prawn and out of curiosity I stop to read his profile. 'Job: chef/part-time model. Interests: weightlifting, rugby, casual sex'. What is Mel doing with this guy? Stupid question.

Jump cut to several days later.

'Where've you been? We were about to give up'.

'Working'. Mel grins and holds out her paint-stained hands, palms up.

'Oh yeah. What are you working on?' Anja asks. She's wearing a long multi-coloured dress. Silver bangles rattle on her arm.

'Jamie'.

'The pr ...' Izzy stops. 'Your man', she says, 'from the dating site?'

'Yeah. He agreed to pose for me. "Quid pro quo", he said. Jesus, you'd want to see him'. Mel flops down on a beanbag next to me.

'What do you mean quid pro quo?'

She glances round, makes sure no one's in earshot and then says, 'In turn I let him take some pictures of me'.

A gasp from Anja. 'Noooo'.

Mel shrugs. 'Why not?'

'Why not?! He could do anything with them, Mel, blackmail ... anything! What if he decided to upload them?'

'Don't be daft', she says, but her face has coloured. 'Besides, I have ...'

'What? A painting? Sure that could be anyone – that's, that's art'.

'So is photography', Anja says. 'Photography is art'.

'Thank you, Anja', Mel mutters. I can see we've set her on edge. In all her blind vanity she clearly overlooked the threat, the fact that she was now in the chef's power.

'Maybe you could get them back?' Anja suggests.

'Wouldn't do any good, he'd have back-ups', I say.

'Jesus, would you stop. You're really freaking me out', Mel takes out her cigarette papers. 'Why was I so fucking stupid?'

Izzy goes to answer but I give her a look that leaves her open-mouthed but silent.

I sip my tea and contemplate. 'Have you been to his place?' I ask.

'Yeah – Tuesday night. It's some kip', she says. 'Bedsit in Rathmines. Has a loft instead of a bedroom'.

'He lives alone then?'

'Yeah. It's one of those big houses divided into self-contained flats. Why?' she asks, curious.

'Maybe we could get them back – the pictures. They're bound to be on his computer, right?'

'I'd never manage that. How would I get out of there with his computer without him seeing me?'

I grin. 'He wouldn't be there, would he? We'd go over when he was working. He's a chef, isn't he? They work till crazy hours of the night'.

Mel is starting to like this plan. I see it in the way her eyes have widened. She looks round. 'Are you saying we break in?'

'Oh, that's kind of a crude way of putting it'. I say.

Anja looks horrified. 'I'm not involved in this', she says, diamond stud twinkling as she shakes her head vigorously.

'Course not. All we need is the two of us'.

Exterior. Evening. Mel and me are sitting on a bench opposite the chef's place, casing the building waiting for our chance. Mel is picking at a thread on her poncho. 'Listen, Jules', she says. 'There's something I have to tell you. I wasn't going to but ...'

I stop her. 'Is this about Paul on that website, because I looked and I couldn't find his profile'.

She nods. 'I just said that to see how you'd take it'.

'What? But why?'

She looks at me. 'Because he *is* seeing someone – and since she hasn't told you, somebody has to'.

I'm staring at her, uncomprehending. 'Anja', she says. 'Pablo's been seeing Anja'.

I laugh, even smack her on the arm. 'That's a good one, Mel', I say, but she isn't smiling. 'I saw them together', she says, 'last week at the cinema. I've been trying to get her to tell you'.

For a minute I think the ground shifts. The camera lurches forward, makes me dizzy. 'Are you sure? You're sure it was Anja?' She nods.

I'm about to mouth an expletive but it dies on my lips as Mel nudges me and the camera swivels to the right in one continuous shot tracking a guy in a blue hoodie heading for the chef's building.

Mel and I both stand and cross the street quickly. The guy in the hoodie holds the door for us assuming we're residents and I smile queasily and thank him. Mel puts her hand on my arm. 'Are you alright?' I nod. Dumb from the news. Now isn't the time and so I block it.

We climb the stairs to the second floor. 'Now what?' Mel hisses as the imaginary camera stops and focuses on the closed door to the chef's apartment, the numbers one and zero in silver letters on the green glossy paint. 'Just as we said', I tell her, 'you hide and I'll find the caretaker'.

It's easier than either of us anticipated. The caretaker's a Romanian guy and I tell him I'm Jamie's sister, that I've lost my key and he won't be home till after midnight. 'You know he's a chef', I say. 'They work till all hours'. I smile then, ask him where he's from, I tell him about my trip the year before around Transylvania, that he has a beautiful country. By the time we reach the prawn's door, I've given him my number – a fake one of course. Mel's been listening from the stairs above. Soon as my Transylvanian friend leaves she skips down. We hurry into the chef's flat and close the door behind us. 'Smooth', she says.

Mel crosses the room and pulls the curtains. She flicks the light switch, illuminating the dingy interior, the flaking paint. 'Right, where do we start?'

'Camera and computer', I tell her. 'People never print things these days'.

The place is such a tip it's hard to know where to start. Clothes and shoes everywhere. Curious, I ascend to the loft – Mel was a bit mean. In theory it is a loft but bigger than what I anticipated.

I pull open a chest of drawers. My hand alights on a long, curly black wig. I draw back, stifle a scream and then realising what it is, take it out and examine it. Mel shouts up from the living room, 'Got the camera. Any sign of the computer?'

When her head appears at the top of the steps I'm standing above her, the black curls falling past my shoulders. 'Holy shit! Where did you get that?' she says. I point at the drawer and break into a bad Cher impersonation. 'Seems there's more to your chef than you realised', I say.

The wig is just the start of it. That chest unearths a whole array of women's accessories. But much more of a concern is the stack of recordable DVDs in the wardrobe.

Freeze frame – Mel's face as she picks up the DVDs and reads one woman's name after another. Freda. Amanda. Zenitha. Her head swivels as she casts about for a camera, a new horror occurring to her.

'Zenitha', I say out loud. 'Wasn't that the name of that Turkish woman who went missing a few months ago?'

Mel gathers a handful of tapes, stuffs them into her oversized handbag. 'The computer', I say, just as we hear the key turning. Mel frantically gestures for me to get down. I scramble behind the bed and she thrusts her bag at me. From beneath the bed I see Mel's ankles. She kicks off her shoes and removes her socks. I hear the rustle of clothes as hurriedly she undresses. The chef is moving about downstairs. For a moment Mel's face appears over the edge of the bed. 'Get out', she hisses, 'soon as you have the chance'. And then the sound of his shoes on the wooden stairs.

'How did you get in?'

Mel stands. I see her bare legs and feet, silver dolphin anklet glinting as she moves towards him. 'Persuaded that caretaker of yours to let me in', she purrs. 'Thought I'd surprise you'.

Zenitha. Amanda. Freda. Names whirling around in my head. Familiar names. Names I've seen in the newspaper in the past two years. Names of the missing.

Sound of metal, a clang as the chef's jeans fall to the floor. Zenitha – her car found in the car park of a Dublin pub. Freda – a German tourist who'd gone for a hike in the Dublin mountains with a meet-up group. She was last spotted getting in a car with a woman with long dark hair.

Mel is cooing above me – a hand falls over the edge of the bed, signalling for me to get out – get out – get out before the picture fades to black and the camera stops spinning.

Marty

Larissa stands at the water's edge. In the silver surface of the lake her reflection sways before her, shimmers like a mirage. She imagines sinking deep down in the dark water, her naked body coming to rest on the stony bed beneath. Rain starts. She turns her face up to feel its cooling effect. Then she turns to the baby. He is still asleep in his pram. She pulls the hood up to protect him but then she turns away again, looks at the clouds gathering overhead threatening a storm.

She comes here at the same time every day, sits on the same park bench and enjoys the silence. Sometimes she watches the other mothers, but she doesn't speak to them. She always looks away just before the point of contact, before the false comparisons begin. Larissa has no interest in other people's babies.

She glances at the boy. He's wrapped safely in his blue rug unaware yet of the world. His sleeping face is peaceful. He's too young to dream. Outside the park there is the distant sound of passing traffic. As the rain becomes heavier she can hear the swish of their tyres on the wet road, all of the people hurrying somewhere. She too begins to move faster, head down, aware only of the baby and the need to get him home. She hopes he won't wake before they reach the house.

The baby is three months old. His name is Marty. It was his grandfather's name and she doesn't care for it, but they agreed that if it was a boy Philip would name him. And if it was a girl she would choose. She wonders if it would've made a difference somehow. If Marty had been Melinda would anything have changed? But inside she knows the answer.

Sometimes she tries to count the days from when she arrived home from the hospital to the current day, but she can't remember how long it's been because every day's the same. Her life before seems like a dream. She has a hazy recollection of business meetings, of days filled with interviewing potential employees, of making decisions, of there never being enough time. Now the days are endless.

Larissa pushes on through the rain. It stings her face like needles. She stops at one point and checks the baby. He's sleeping soundly, his face turned slightly to the side. His cheek is soft against the pillow. Sometimes she worries that he sleeps too soundly. She stands at the foot of the cot for long periods of time just to make sure he's breathing. Then she asks herself how she'd feel if he wasn't and quickly tries to banish the evil thought from her mind.

At eleven o'clock the phone rings. She's expecting the call but she's in the middle of heating Marty's bottle. She curses as she sloshes some milk on the counter then struggles with the top and curses again. Marty's awake now. He's watching her with round eyes, blue eyes like his father's. She puts the bottle in the microwave. Then runs for the phone.

She picks up, slightly breathless and hears Philip's voice at the other end. She feels relief and resentment at once and she cannot explain these emotions.

'Hi baby, it's me. Is everything ok?'

'Sure, everything's fine', she says.

She smiles because she believes you can hear a smile as well as see it. And maybe he will believe that what she says is true.

'How's Marty?' he says.

'Marty's great. He's sleeping. We've just been to the park'.

In the background she hears voices. Telephones ring and are answered. She pictures an office full of people. She imagines Philip in his swivel chair, his photograph of her and Marty on the desk and she envies him.

'And how are you, baby? Are you alright?'

Her eyes well up and she wipes them with the back of her hand. She doesn't even know why she's crying. She's never been like this before.

'Of course, I'm fine, sweetie. How's work? Are you busy?'

She tries to sound bright. The baby is watching her with big accusing eyes. The microwave bleeps in the background to tell her that the bottle is heated. She tries to block out the sound, to concentrate on what Philip is saying. As she listens, she watches Marty. She sees his mouth opening for a millisecond before the screaming begins. His eyes widen and he digs his tiny fists into his eyes and kicks his feet, which poke out from under the blue blanket. She doesn't hear Philip's reply.

'I'm sorry Phil. Marty's awake now. I'll have to go', she says.

She wants to get off the phone before he hears the screaming. She wants him to think that she's doing ok, that she's not a bad mother. She doesn't consider the fact that it's natural for babies to cry, that he does it three times a night and Philip gets out of bed to feed him. She wonders why Philip reacts so differently. Why he's so much better at this than her.

She hangs up the phone. Then burns her hand with the baby's bottle, which has been left in the microwave for too long. The baby screams louder, his face turning scarlet, spittle running down his chin. She cools the milk and sucks at the teat to make sure that the temperature's ok. Marty's tiny hands reach out greedily to grip the bottle. As soon as she gives it to him the howling stops. He lies there sucking at the bottle, his eyes closed in contentment. Larissa sits on the sofa with the baby on her knee. She wipes the moisture from under his eyes and dabs at the tears that have already begun to dry on his cheeks. When she looks at him she feels nothing and she hates herself for feeling this way.

Philip has installed baby monitors in every room in the house. Everywhere Larissa goes she can hear Marty. When she puts him down to sleep she sits on the sofa and closes her eyes and tries to relax but her heart is beating fast and she finds herself listening to every sound coming from the monitor instead. There are times when she can't hear anything and that is worse. She checks that it's switched on and hurries to the baby's room to watch him with her own eyes, suspicious of the capabilities of modern technology.

When Philip comes home from work the first thing he does is kiss Larissa, then he plucks Marty from his cot and swings him high in the air.

'How's my boy?' he says.

Larissa smiles, but her smile is empty.

She heats Philip's dinner in the microwave, takes it out of the cellophane and cooks it on full power. She hasn't cooked a proper meal in days. She tells him that she's already eaten. She has no appetite and doesn't want him fussing about her health. She knows that she's lost weight. Her trousers are loose on her hips and she has to wear a belt to keep them up. This morning she had to make a new hole in the belt. She took a screwdriver and drove it through the leather before tightening it round her waist. I'm fading away, she thinks. She wonders if it's possible to fade to nothing, disappear into the ether. A speck of dust on the universe.

After dinner Philip gives the baby a bath. Larissa stands in the doorway and watches. Philip has his shirt sleeves rolled up to his elbows, but they are still wet. A dark patch stains his light blue shirt across the front but he doesn't seem to notice. He's busy soaping Marty's head. Marty splashes in the water and laughs. He looks like a baby on an advert, all smiles and bubbles. Philip turns away as the water splashes him some more.

'Hey watch it!' he says.

Marty gurgles and smiles. Larissa watches and wonders what's wrong with her? They would be better off without me, she thinks as she watches her husband and son.

That night Larissa lies in bed and cannot sleep. She stares at the ceiling and tries to make out shapes in the darkness of the room. There is a tall dark shape looming where the chest of drawers stands in daylight. It looks like a person lurking in the corner of the room and for some reason it makes Larissa think of her father and the last time she saw him with a suitcase in his hand, his big frame silhouetted in the doorway of her and her sister's room before he disappeared into the night.

As Larissa lies there she hears Marty moving in his cot at the end of the bed and she feels her body tense up in anticipation. He begins to whimper like a small animal waking from sleep. Then it becomes a full-blown cry and

Philip stirs in the bed beside her. His foot brushes against her as he sits up and swings his legs over the edge. She feels the cold night air creeping beneath the duvet as he moves but she stays perfectly still.

'It's ok, I'm coming', Philip says.

His voice is low, conspiratorial as he speaks to his son in the dark. She sees him as he leans low over the cot and takes the baby in his arms. They make just one figure, man and son, as Larissa watches them quietly from the bed.

'It's ok, little man'.

He hushes the baby with quiet words. She listens to his voice in the dark, a voice that has spoken to her, in the night, with equal tenderness. Philip rocks the baby as he moves about the room searching for something, his slippers perhaps. He knocks against the dressing table and her bottles of perfume shudder but continue to stand upright. She knows each sound by memory, pictures the bottles, like sentries, lined up before the mirror.

For a short while they are gone. She lies there in the silence and imagines them in the other room, Philip organising things so carefully. Then they return. She hears Marty sucking at his bottle, feels the weight at her feet as Philip sits on the end of the bed pinning her to the mattress. The rain has started again. It pounds at the window. Instinctively she tries to pull the duvet up around her, but it doesn't budge under Philip's weight. She pictures herself outside in the rain, her face upturned, the drops soaking through her nightclothes, running down her legs to her bare feet. She imagines running far, far away from here, a shadowy figure absorbed into the night.

Instead she lies there, cold, listening to Marty sucking at his bottle and to Philip whispering in the dark. Finally Philip stands and she pulls the covers higher. He leans down, tucking Marty back into his cot. He is sleeping now. She hears his soft baby breaths.

Philip climbs into bed beside her bringing with him the cold night air. She lies on her back and he moves in towards her. He puts an arm around her body and she cannot move. 'I'm like my father', she thinks. For a moment she wonders if she's said the words out loud, Philip groans a sort of questioning sound, but then he turns over and sleeps, leaving her to the night.

At dawn Larissa rises. She is in the kitchen scrambling eggs when Philip appears in the kitchen doorway.

'Hey, what's this?' he says.

'I thought I'd make us breakfast'. She smiles brightly, stirs the contents of the saucepan with a wooden spoon. There's bacon and sausages on a plate under the grill. She has a window open to let out the smoke and a cold wind moves the curtain.

'It smells great'.

Philip smiles and knots his tie as Larissa continues to work with her back to him. Through the monitor she can hear the sound of Marty sleeping, his soft baby sighs. When the food is done, Larissa sits at the table across from her husband. It is the first meal she's shared with him in some time. She feels his eyes on her as she eats and she looks at her plate as she cuts the food up into small pieces before chewing them slowly and swallowing them down with a mouthful of tea.

Philip reads yesterday's paper. He stops every now and then to tell her about some story he's reading. He reads her an excerpt, then continues on. Now and then she makes a comment and he looks up from the paper and smiles. It's like it used to be, the two of them together, only she can hear Marty in the background, a third entity.

Philip kisses her at the door. She kisses him back and he lingers in the hallway until she pushes him away.

'Let's go to bed', he says.

She laughs. 'Go!' she tells him.

He kisses her again, then takes his briefcase and leaves the house. He's smiling as he goes.

Larissa clears away the plates. She scrapes the remains into the bin and washes the dishes beneath the hot tap. She picks up a mug with her lipstick on the rim, then leaves it down again and dries her hands in the teacloth.

In the bedroom Marty stirs. She gives him his formula and he sucks at the bottle, half-asleep, half-awake. He is not due another feed yet, but she has given him something to keep him asleep, something to calm him. She kisses his forehead, tucks the blanket round him and shuts the door as she leaves the room.

Outside the sky is still dark. Rain-clouds hang low over the horizon. Larissa hurries down the street, the hood of her blue anorak pulled over her head. To the passers-by she looks like a woman racing against the imminent rainstorms, but instead she is racing towards them. She enters the park, makes her way along the pathway that winds through the trees. On a bench a man is sleeping, his blue-green sleeping bag pulled up over his head so that she cannot see his face. He doesn't move as she passes.

Larissa follows the path until she comes to the lake. Then she stands at the edge and stares into the water. She picks up a stone, arcs her arm and flings it into the water. It disappears with a plop. She strains to see it as it sinks beneath the surface but the water is dark, reflecting the sky and it is impossible to see the bottom of the lake. Only the ripples on the surface remain.

As Larissa enters the water she sees an image of her husband, his face up close as he kissed her goodbye. She steps down the bank fully clothed and feels the thrill of the icy water as it fills her boots. Her clothes become sodden as she is dragged deeper and deeper below the surface. She tries to open her eyes to look at the sky but it's impossible. As the water closes over her, Larissa thinks she hears a baby crying. She opens her mouth to scream 'Marty' but her words are just bubbles on the water's surface.

My Brother Adam

Adam sat in his usual chair beneath the window. Late afternoon sun poured through the glass illuminating the room and making his pale skin seem even whiter than it was. It had only been three weeks since I started visiting him in this room, yet everything was familiar to me. I knew the way the light landed on the far wall at this time of day and the shapes of the shadows cast upon the floor. I knew the way that Adam had of simply sitting there staring out through the window, his eyes vacant, as though he didn't see anything on the other side.

He looked up as we entered. There were days when he didn't hear me come into the room so absorbed was he with his thoughts, but today I brought Amy and her tiny shoes made a racket on the tiled floor as she skipped by my side. Despite her skipping she held my hand tightly as though she sensed that there was something unpleasant about the place, something that made her cease the bird-like chatter that kept me distracted all the way down here in the car.

When Adam saw us he smiled slightly and straightened in his chair. On the bed next to where he sat a tray held the remnants of his afternoon meal. It was good to see that he was eating again. Consciously I chalked it down as a sign that the nurse was right about him improving. I needed clarification, a guarantee. I had told her this, this morning when she called but she argued and told me that there were no guarantees. People, she said, were not despatched with warranties.

'Did you bring the paper?' Adam asked, before I had a chance to sit down.

'Sure', I said. I handed him *The Irish Times*. He took the newspaper from me, mumbled his thanks and began to look through it. I watched anxiously as he scanned the pages, turning them rapidly as though he were searching for something in particular. He stopped to read a short article.

'Was there something special you wanted to see?' I asked.

'No, nothing', he said. He closed the paper and threw it on the bed. Then he leaned across and took a box of Cadbury's Roses from the bedside locker.

'Would you like one?' he asked.

He held the box out to Amy but she shied away, shook her head and hid behind my chair. She was afraid of her uncle Adam. He usually didn't speak to her. Amy found this strange because people were always making a fuss of her. The last time she'd seen her uncle he'd shouted at her granny and made her cry. She wasn't used to people shouting. Gerry and I tried to shield her from this as much as we could. If we had a disagreement, it was something that was dealt with after bedtime, never in front of the child.

Adam didn't register Amy's reaction. It didn't occur to him that he was someone to fear. He took a sweet from the box, unwrapped it and popped it into his mouth. These sweets were his favourites because they were wrapped in coloured foil and could not have been contaminated by the nurses. When he was first admitted he refused to eat anything. He was convinced that the hospital staff were trying to poison him. 'I know what you're trying to do', he'd said. They continued to bring him his meals and he continued to leave them untouched, coagulating on the plate until they looked as unpalatable as he imagined they were. That first week I brought him chicken sandwiches, carefully wrapped in tin foil, which he eyed suspiciously before deciding, for whatever reason, that I was someone who wished him no harm. Then he ate as though it were his last meal.

'How are you feeling today?' I asked.

'Great', he said. He looked away again, stared past me out of the window and into the grounds where other patients sat on wooden benches talking or smoking or simply staring into a world that only they could see. 'Listen, I'm sorry about what happened …' he said. 'I know that you're trying to help me …'

I nodded, embarrassed at his sudden disclosure. We hadn't spoken about it in the three weeks that he had been here. I didn't know how to bring it up. A part of me was afraid to mention that night. I didn't know what way he would react. He might try to defend his actions. And if he did, then I knew that I couldn't be the one to take care of him.

'Adam …' I said.

He looked at me, then suddenly rose and tightened the belt of his oversized hospital dressing gown. 'God, I'm dying for a cigarette', he said.

I nodded. Relieved at the temporary reprieve he had given me.

He took a packet of cigarette papers and tobacco from the pocket of the gown. I stood up and took Amy by the hand. My eyes strayed to the hospital logo embroidered on his left breast, an insurance against patients checking out early. That and a pair of pyjamas were the only things that they had to wear. Both were too big for my brother's narrow frame.

It was a relief to be outside. We sat on a bench in the dying sun while Amy played in the grass nearby scooping up the autumn leaves and letting them fall around her like confetti. I watched as Adam began to roll a cigarette, carefully placing the tobacco inside the paper. Nearby an elderly woman moved slowly across the grass. Her daughter walked by her side, her arm under the older woman's elbow offering support. I looked at Adam. His eyes followed the two women as he rolled the cigarette. I wondered what he was thinking. Whether, like me, the old woman reminded him of our mother. He had not asked about her yet. And I didn't dare mention her name.

'They say I might be out next week', he said. He tried to sound casual, finished rolling his cigarette and ran his tongue along the seal, deftly sticking the paper as though he were preparing to post a letter. My mouth was dry. 'Maybe Tuesday, it depends …' he said.

I looked away then, searched for the right words. Instead, I simply nodded. It was too soon. I needed time to decide, it would not be right to raise his expectations. Adam was my only sibling and yet a selfish part of me was reluctant to accept responsibility for him. I had a family of my own, a little girl who I wanted to protect against all harm and a husband who did not sign up for this. Gerry said he didn't mind, that whatever decision I made he would support it. Yet how could I expect him to shoulder a burden that I was so hesitant to undertake?

'How's Mam?' He blurted it suddenly, a child in need of reassurance. His eyes pleaded for understanding. The unlit cigarette dangled between his fingers, crushed slightly from the strength of his grip.

'Coping', I said.

He nodded, took a lighter from the pocket of his dressing gown and put the cigarette between his lips. I was not ready to forgive him. But I didn't want to hurt him with the truth. I didn't mention her refusal to visit, though he would've noticed that by now. Or that she couldn't stop crying, wondering why her youngest child hated her so much. She didn't understand that Adam was ill. She thought that somehow it was her fault. That she had failed as a mother. I watched as Adam closed his eyes, inhaled deeply and exhaled the smoke through his nostrils and despite the effort I was trying to make to put it all behind me I recalled the events of that night.

Gerry had called to say that he was working late. So I decided to take Amy and go over to see my mother. Amy was excited about seeing her granny on a weeknight. Usually we didn't get a chance to visit until the weekend. I still had a set of keys to my mother's house and I always let myself in. It saved her from having to get up to answer the door. She was not so good on her feet. As soon as I stepped into the hall that evening I heard Adam's voice. He was talking in high-pitched tones. Then I heard my mother.

'No, no!' she said.

I rushed into the living room. My mother was in an armchair, slunk down low in the seat. Adam stood over her. A standing lamp was poised in his hand, raised well above his shoulder and he was shouting at her.

'I know what you're trying to do', he said. 'You're all in this together ...'

'Adam'. I screamed his name and he turned, surprised. He lowered the lamp and I rushed towards him and snatched it from his hand. He just stared.

'What are you doing?' I said.

He looked at me for a minute as though he didn't know me. Then he shook his head and pointed at my mother who was still cowering in the chair, terrified.

'She's putting stuff in my food', he said. 'She's trying to poison me. She thinks I don't know what she's doing ... but I know alright ... I know ...' His voice rose as he spoke.

I stood between him and my mother and he stepped backwards, looking confused. I sat on the arm of the chair and put my arms around her. Her shoulders were shaking. I had forgotten about Amy standing behind me. She stood there staring as her grandmother tried to hold back the tears springing from her eyes. Adam left the room. I heard his footsteps hurrying up the stairs and the sound of his bedroom door slamming.

That was when my mother told me the other things. How Adam thought that the world was conspiring against him. He had not opened his bedroom curtains for weeks because he was convinced that the man who lived across the street was watching him. He stumbled about in the dark, refusing even to turn on a light. For Adam, any little movement made by another person was read as a signal. The slightest thing, a girl flicking her hair over her shoulder as she stood at a bus stop, meant much more to him than to anyone else. That night my mother admitted that there was something wrong with my brother.

Adam and I sat in silence for some time. He continued to smoke but didn't ask any more questions. I watched my little girl sitting in the grass playing with the leaves. At that moment she was oblivious to us, absorbed only in her own world. I remembered Adam when he was that age. I used to walk him to school, my arm about his shoulders wanting only to protect him, my little brother. His world was not so different from Amy's. It was a world where it was difficult to separate make-believe from truth. But it was a darker world than I hoped my child's would ever be.

I pictured Adam, five years old, laughing as I chased him through the fallen leaves, his fair hair blowing in the breeze. I saw my mother sitting on a park bench smiling at us both as we played. Then I pictured Adam climbing on her knee, arms outstretched reaching up for her to help him.

He sat at my side now, staring into a world that I could never see. I reached out and touched his arm. He looked at me, startled, brought back momentarily from that other place.

'Stay with me, Adam', I said.

He nodded, pulled at his dressing gown and smiled slightly.

'Stay with me'.

WHITEOUT

Lucille left one cold night in December. Her departure was not planned. It was something done in haste as many things in Lucille's life were. That night she had gone to the theatre. She had asked Eugene to accompany her. He was too busy, he said. She didn't mind. She was accustomed to Eugene's refusal, particularly of late, when it seemed impossible to persuade him out of doors. Besides, she liked to go out alone. It gave her an air of mystery.

It was late when she got home. He had left the light on downstairs for her. It shone through the hall window, illuminated the concrete figures in the neighbour's garden, lending them a somewhat eerie appearance, like apparitions, white and still. Lucille pulled into the garage. She switched the engine off and rummaged in her bag for the key. She opened the door and stepped into the hall. She plucked at the fingers of her leather gloves and unwound the scarf from around her neck. She hung her red coat on the end of the banister, sat on the stairs and pulled her boots off.

She wondered whether Eugene had gone to bed. She felt a thrill at the prospect. She would creep upstairs, slip beneath the covers and wake him to make love. It was a game they often played. In the dark she could be anyone. Her lips travelling down his body could be those of a stranger. She thought of him stirring in half-sleep, his body responding to her touch. The thought that it might not be her partner in the bed, but instead a complete stranger was an erotic if slim possibility. Lucille had a taste for the dramatic.

She laid her keys and bag on the living room table where an open bottle of red wine stood, uncorked. Beside it, a glass that was not quite empty. Lucille raised the glass to her lips and drained it. Her lipstick stained the rim red. She poured herself another, lingered in the living room. She sat on the sofa and put her feet up on the wooden table. It had been a good show. She was sorry that Eugene had not gone with her. He liked that type of thing. Lately, all he ever seemed to do was work. Still, once the book was finished, she supposed, everything could get back to normal.

Lucille finished her wine. She left her glass on the table and turned the light out. Slowly she climbed the stairs. The bedroom door was closed. She eased it open and stepped inside. Eugene's shaving lotion spiked the air. She guessed that he was not long gone to bed. In the dark she undressed and hung her clothes over the arm of the bedroom chair.

'How was the show?'

She was surprised when he spoke. She figured that he would be asleep or pretending to be asleep.

'It was good, very good. You'd have liked it', she said.

Lucille stood on one foot, then the other, as she peeled off her tights and flung them on the chair. She slipped beneath the covers. Eugene's body was warm. His hair was damp from the shower. She waited for him to turn toward her. When he didn't she wondered whether he had fallen asleep. She began to feel slightly annoyed. Not only had her fantasy been dashed, he made no attempt to touch her. She lay on her back. There was a gap between their bodies which she refused to close. Eugene had pulled the pillows down at an angle and was curled away from her toward the wall. Cold crept beneath the covers. She sighed. She was tired and irritable.

'I was talking to Amy', Eugene's voice rang out in the silence. He was not asleep after all.

'Oh. How is she?'

'She's fine'. He paused. 'I told her to come over at the weekend'.

'What's she coming over here for?' she said. The words were out before she could stop them. She hated this, hated the way she sounded, even though she knew that she had good reason. She always ended up sounding unreasonable, irrational even. And she hated that.

'Are you in a mood?' He hadn't moved. His words were muffled beneath the blankets.

'No. I'm just asking what she's coming over here for, that's all'.

'Why wouldn't she?' he said.

She lay on her back, her eyes adjusted now to the darkness. 'Well, you needn't expect me to entertain her', she said.

'Nobody's expecting you to do anything'.

And that was that. Lucille waited, thinking that maybe still he might turn toward her. She wouldn't touch him, not now. She would not make the first move. She lay on her back and waited. He said nothing more. In the silence her irritation grew. It was fuelled by the fact that he did nothing to pacify her, nothing to comfort her. She thought that the move to Edmonton might have changed things, that the distance might have proved too great for their friendship to endure.

She lay there and wondered what to do. She couldn't sleep. Her mind was too active. She wished that he would say something. Anything. That way they could have it out and be done with it. Eugene said nothing. Lucille turned over, widening the void. She could sleep downstairs, she supposed, on the sofa. That would make a statement. Or she could leave. The thought occurred to her suddenly. She didn't know why. But now that it had occurred she couldn't rest easy. She felt that she had no choice. That is what she would do – she would leave. It wouldn't get that far anyway. Eugene would ask her what she was doing as soon as he heard her stumbling around in the dark. He would tell her not to be foolish, to come back to bed. Eugene was practical like that.

Lucille slipped from beneath the covers. She sat on the edge of the bed. She was tired, too tired for such foolishness. She stood up. She tripped on his boots in the dark and cursed softly. That would wake him, if he were not still awake. She took her clothes from the bedroom chair. She dressed and fumbled on the floor for her shoes. She sat on the edge of the bed. Still, he said nothing. Lucille hesitated. Was he asleep after all? Time was running out. Maybe she should get undressed, slip into bed and say nothing, but she had come this far.

She stood up. Noisily, she opened the bedroom door. The figure beneath the clothes did not stir. She closed the door behind her and crept down the stairs. She stopped in the hall, sat down on the bottom step of the stairs and waited. The only sound was the ticking of the clock. God, she was tired. Her eyes burned when she closed them. Perhaps she would go for a walk as far as the garden gate. She dare not go any further, not with the forecast.

She took her keys from the table and opened the front door. Moonlight filled the hallway. Lucille stepped outside and pulled the door behind her. It was cold. Damn cold. Frost shimmered dangerously on the pavement. The snow had not yet come. She moved her feet, rubbed her arms. She watched the front door, which remained maddeningly closed. Then she had an idea.

She opened the garage door, unlocked the car and sat into the driver's seat. She put the key in the ignition. What if he looked out and the car was gone? He would be frantic. He would come after her surely? What man wouldn't? And so Lucille had her plan. She would drive to the end of the road and stop there. She would wait a few minutes. That was all it would take for him to arrive.

She started the engine. She turned the heater on and gripped the wheel. She reversed out of the drive and put the car into gear. Slowly, she pulled away from the house. She glanced in the rear view mirror. Nothing stirred. She rounded the bend, continued on for a couple of blocks and then pulled in. She turned the lights off, but left the engine running. There was nobody around. Houses were in darkness, their inhabitants fast asleep. Lucille looked at the sky. A full moon illuminated the night. A cat streaked across the road and disappeared into somebody's garden. Suddenly, she felt alone. She locked the car doors and sat back in her seat. Every so often she glanced up the road.

Lucille switched the radio on. She drummed her fingers on the steering wheel. She was beginning to feel foolish. What must he think after all? She wondered about Amy. Had she phoned? Had he phoned her? What difference did it make? She had taken a dislike to the woman. It wasn't the fact that they were close, though that did have something to do with it. She couldn't stand her whining voice or the way she pawed him when she spoke. He, of course, never noticed. Or he pretended not to. They had been friends for years, he and Amy. She was the first girl he had slept with. A brief adolescent fling – it was something that Amy liked to joke about in an all-too-innocent way. It made Lucille smoulder.

She looked at the dashboard. The needle on the fuel gauge hovered just above empty. The yellow warning light was on. Her eyes were heavy with sleep. She flicked through the radio channels, looked for something that might keep her awake until he came. 'Minus thirty-eight degrees tonight in Edmonton and falling', she was in time to hear the announcer say. She turned the heat up. In the mirror, she saw a car approaching. The lights vanished at the bend and then re-appeared. Her heart quickened. The car approached slowly. She waited for the driver to indicate and pull in. Instead, they drove on. Lucille slumped forward in her seat, gripped the steering wheel and laid her head against her hands. The engine spluttered and then died. She tried to start it. It moaned. The yellow light blinked at her.

Cold crept into the car and she tightened her scarf beneath her collar. Her fingers were numb in the leather gloves. She wriggled them, rubbed her hands together in an attempt to circulate the blood. She thought of Eugene, his body warm against hers as they lay parallel between the sheets. She shivered and drew her coat closer round her. There was not a sound. Not a sign of life. Lucille watched the road. A flake drifted and stuck to the windscreen. Another followed it. Soon it began to come down heavily. Snowflakes whirled and stuck to the glass. She turned the wipers on. She couldn't see a damn thing. She couldn't feel her feet now. Her cuffs were pulled over her hands. Every so often she thought she heard a car and glanced eagerly toward the bend. Lights appeared in the distance and vanished. Lucille's eyes closed. It became more of an effort to open them each time, her lids were so heavy. Her head drifted sideways, rested against the window. She was vaguely aware of the cold glass against her skin, like metal. Lucille waited. Her eyes closed. This time she did not bother to open them. She was tired, too tired for such foolishness. Lucille slept. Eugene dreamed. The forecaster's voice crackled over the airwaves. Whiteout.

Acknowledgments

Many thanks to the editors and judges who have published and given awards to earlier versions of these stories: 'When Black Dogs Sing' won runner-up prize in the William Trevor competition and was published in *Crannog* and in *Bray Arts Journal;* 'The Prodigal' was shortlisted for the RTÉ Francis Mac Manus Award, 2015 and published in *The Incubator Journal*; 'What Happened at the Clarkes' was published on *Headstuff.org*; 'Shadows' was published in *The Sunday Tribune*/Hennessy New Irish Writing Awards, 2002; 'Why, Molly?' received an honourable mention in The Lorian Hemmingway competition, 2015; 'The Fever' was published in *The Cúirt Annual* and received an honourable mention in the *Aesthetica* short story competition, 2007; 'Where Did You Go?' was shortlisted for the 2002 RTÉ Francis Mac Manus Awards and published in *Whispers and Shouts*. In 2016 'The Pilgrimage' was published in *Southlight* magazine and shortlisted for the Galway Rape Crisis Centre's short story competition, 2015; 'Saying Goodbye to Bettina' received an honourable mention in the Limnisa competition, 2010; 'By the River's Edge' won runner-up prize in the Trevor/Bowen short story competition; 'Counting Stars' was published in West47 online; 'The Picnic' was shortlisted for The Cúirt New Writing Prize 2015; 'Marty' was longlisted in 2008 for the Fish competition as 'Ophelia in the Park'; 'My Brother Adam' was published in the *Cúirt Annual,* 2007; 'Whiteout' was published in *Cúirt 21* and won second prize in the Maria Edgeworth competition in 2002.

Special thanks are due to Alan Hayes whose dedication to the discovery and publication of fresh voices in Irish literature is unparalleled. And to Tom Gallagher for all those Wednesday books that fuelled my imagination. Thanks to my brother, Trevor, for both his encouragement and belief. And to my 'forever friend' Antoinette McGough, and sister-in-law, Daniela Cabral for being so lovely. Thanks to Keith Burke for his recording of *Exposed* and for his valued friendship over the years. Thanks to my ISI family and their support. Thank you to the readers and writers who have appreciated my work. A huge thank you to my husband, David Butler – and to Dave O'Keeffe, the matchmaker. Above all, thank you to my mother. We love and miss her every day.

About the Author

Tanya Farrelly works as an EFL teacher, and facilitates creative writing classes for South Dublin County Council. Her stories have won prizes and been shortlisted in such competitions as the Hennessy Awards, the RTÉ Francis Mac Manus Awards (2002/2015), Fish and the Cúirt New Writing Prize. Runner-up in the William Trevor International Short Story Competition in both 2008 and 2009, her stories have appeared in literary journals such as the *Cúirt Annual, Crannog* magazine and the Incubator Journal. Her debut novel *The Girl Behind the Lens* is being published by Harper Collins on 28 October 2016. Tanya is also the founder of Staccato Spoken Word event.